TAP DANCE

Tap Dance

A TALL TALE OF THE WILD WEST

Robert S. Levinson

THORNDIKE PRESS
A part of Gale, a Cengage Company

GALE
A Cengage Company

LIBRARY OF CONGRESS CIP DATA ON FILE.
CATALOGUING IN PUBLICATION FOR THIS BOOK
IS AVAILABLE FROM THE LIBRARY OF CONGRESS

ISBN-13: 978-1-4328-5496-6 (hardcover alk. paper)

Published in 2020 by arrangement with Robert Levinson

Printed in Mexico
Print Number: 01   Print Year: 2020

To Bob
This one is for you
LVY

In Memoriam
1936–2018

"Events make history. It's the retelling that makes heroes."

—Ned Buchanan

"Facts are what we believe. Truths are what we know."

—Ruben Garner

CHAPTER 1

Anytime the old memories come back to me, Swaney and McDukes are alive again, beating leather west of the ninety-eighth meridian. I'm a youngster again. My thinning white hair an unruly red. No liver freckles or veins marring my pale white skin. Muscles tight. Belly hard and flat. Eyesight sharp as cactus needles. A passion for hard liquor, soft women, and oversized Havanas.

In those memories, the magic sunshine of electricity hasn't yet made it past the Rockies. The territories are still lit by oil lamps and dreams of a better, richer life that preempt the reality of day-to-day survival. It's a time when what happened is worse than what did not. It's a place where people killed to live and lived to kill.

I could list the names here.

And the inventions.

And the truths.

I won't, except for some.

Mainly for Swaney and McDukes.

Everything worth telling begins with them.

Everybody knows their legend.

Not everybody knows the truth.

I'm one of the few who does, starting that first day they met inside the tall walls of Desert Prison.

The old converted fort was the only stronghold with a fair chance of containing them.

McDukes arrived with other ideas.

He got in to get Swaney out.

A good thing Swaney wanted out or one of them would have been dead before too many more sunsets lit up the horizon line.

Swaney had three years remaining on his seven-year sentence and was king of the yard by the time McDukes arrived, was processed, and went looking for his old running mate. Two weeks after landing at the prison, Swaney had taken the title away from Bill "The Butcher" Barton in a brief encounter at the seat of power, a courtyard bench by some kind of fruit tree that never bore fruit. In two weeks he'd learned how the system worked, who among the inmates he could win to his side, and what guards were corrupt and could be bought off with sex and smoking tobacco.

The Butcher had ruled longer than any inmate before him, going back more than a dozen years to his first day behind bars, when he tracked the reigning boss, George Drummond, to his cell and without so much as a "good morning" choked the life from him, yanked Drummond's ears from his head, flung them into the toilet bowl, and flushed them away.

It was the Butcher's way of announcing: *I'm the new king around here. Listen to me and obey me or you'll be breathing your last before you know it.*

The Butcher had a good twenty years and thirty pounds on Swaney, as well as a dozen loyal prisoners surrounding him and a carving knife hidden up his sleeve. Word was out and, when Swaney arrived at the fruit tree, the yard was jam-packed with vigorous betting going on, the Butcher a 10-1 favorite.

Swaney saw the danger signs that even a blind man would notice, but was undismayed as he approached the Butcher. Swaney nodded and smiled. The Butcher acknowledged the nod with one of his own, but didn't smile.

"Name's Swaney," Swaney said, his voice mellow as a lullaby. "Lowell Swaney."

The Butcher said nothing.

"I hear this ornery fruit tree used to be yours."

The Butcher, never one for word games, said, "Mean to keep it that way."

"Can't be two kings, can there now, Mr. Barton?"

"Owney one and it ain't ever gonna be you know who," the Butcher said. Grim-faced, he pulled out his carving knife.

It was too late to do him any good.

Swaney moved his arm up and down. The Derringer pistol hidden up his sleeve slipped into his hand. He squeezed the trigger. His shot caught the Butcher in the chest. The Butcher fell to the ground, lifeless eyes staring at the overcast sky.

"Anyone want to dispute the outcome, now's the time," Swaney said.

No challengers emerged before a cadre of guards arrived, some to cart the Butcher's body away, the others to take Swaney into custody and lead him out of the courtyard.

Laws being what they are behind prison bars, the killing cost Swaney a month in solitary on a diet of bread, water, and stale cheese.

His first day out, Swaney headed straight for the courtyard, settled onto the bench by the fruit tree, and stretched his legs, all the declaration he needed to remind everyone he was the new king.

No one came forward to dispute the claim.

Swaney had always been a loner, never went out of his way to make friends and rarely encouraged company.

McDukes's appearance was uninvited and caught him by surprise.

"I come to pay my respects," McDukes said, approaching the bench.

The two men could have been brothers from all appearances, except McDukes was blonder and had burning cobalt-blue eyes that checked out every direction at once. Swaney had immobile coal-black eyes to go with his coal-black shag of hair, and wore a full beard where McDukes was always clean-shaven.

Both stood shy of six-feet, tall for the time, strong-bodied, and handsome in a way that had special appeal for the ladies, McDukes at thirty-one or thirty-two years of age, Swaney about the same age, but seeming a good ten years older because of his darker demeanor.

Swaney studied McDukes, first with one eye and then the other, squinting in the bright sunlight. "Come to kill me, is that what really has you here, McDukes?"

"Nothing much respectful about that, Lowell," McDukes said, rebuking the idea with a smile and a wink. "Only came around to congratulate you on your tree."

Swaney held on to his squint.

By now the courtyard was filling with convicts brought over by the grapevine, sensing a showdown was brewing, odds opening at even money in the betting pool hastily organized by the prison guards.

"I've had better trees," Swaney said.

"Me, also, which may be why this one holds no special interest for yours truly."

"Shame, McDukes. I was fixing to offer you the comfort of this here creaky old wooden bench and what little shade my tree has to offer. Next time, maybe?"

"Sounds good to me," McDukes said, and turned to leave.

"See you, McDukes," Swaney called after him,

"Expect so, Lowell," McDukes answered over his shoulder.

And that was that.

At least, for the time being.

The inmates dispersed, grumbling disappointment.

The guards kept the betting pool open, reckoning Swaney was bound to face another challenge soon, now that McDukes had opened Desert Prison to that possibility. If not him, someone else with a hankering to possess the courtyard bench by the old fruit tree.

McDukes stayed the leading candidate, but only for another six weeks, until the killer Grief Bonner joined the convict population.

Shortly after settling into prison routine, Bonner, built like a buffalo, came running like one at Swaney. He hadn't announced his intentions to capture the tree, but the convict wireless had been buzzing for days about such inevitability. After all, this was the feared Grief Bonner, who had brought pain and suffering, misery and death, to countless Plains families over the years.

Swaney was ready for him.

He sidestepped out of Bonner's path, answering the charge with a hard blow to the neck as Bonner passed him.

Bonner skidded to a stop, hands comforting his throat, and wheeled around, intending to mount a second charge.

Swaney hurriedly moved on him, getting close enough to direct a fist straight into Bonner's beefy midsection. Bonner's hands dropped to his belly. Swaney kicked him in the groin. Bonner howled and moved his hands there protectively as he doubled over in pain. Swaney chopped at Bonner's spine

15

and sent him to the ground. He kicked Bonner in the temple. Then, again. Then, a third time. Bonner's shrieks turned to screams before he grew silent. His body stopped jerking, twitching a bit before it quit moving altogether. He had breathed his last.

Swaney crossed back to his bench, casually, as if returning from a summer stroll.

His convict audience disbanded, those few who had bet on Swaney all smiles, ignoring the grumbling among those who had figured Bonner to win. The guards who showed up to cart Bonner away ignored Swaney, acting as if Bonner had suffered a fatal heart attack. Or something like that.

McDukes waited until they were gone to wander over to Swaney for his first visit since he had arrived at Desert Prison and made his presence known. He had been keeping his distance until the time for them to escape drew closer.

"You surely haven't lost your touch, Lowell," he said.

"Seems so, McDukes."

"You ever consider leaving the tree and moving on?"

"Maybe when I'm ready and feel the urge strong enough."

"Maybe that'll be soon, then."

"You telling me something I should know?

16

Come sit a spell and we'll talk some."

McDukes swung his head left and right. "Time and place for everything, Lowell. Now's neither," he said, and retreated, joining a cluster of convicts across the yard who were discussing female anatomy and similar luxuries of freedom.

McDukes enjoyed the company of other prisoners. They liked him, too, for the sparks of charm and good cheer he threw off, so unlike the brooding and ever melancholy Swaney. Several times he'd been approached about taking on the king of the yard. He treated the suggestion like a joke, explaining he was a man of peace, so long as peace was returned in kind.

Frank Maelstrom, hearing this for the first time, figured McDukes's words for a coward's excuse and told him so. "I'm saying to your face, McDukes, the only notches on your gun belt were ones put there in Beadle dime weeklies, where I first come across your name and your so-called reputation for heroic exploits."

"Suits me fine, Frank."

"That all you got to say for yourself?"

The answer just slipped out: "Maybe also that I'm surprised to hear you can read."

Maelstrom gave him an ugly stare. "You gonna regret saying that," he said, and tramped off.

The prisoners waited for him to leave the courtyard before cautioning McDukes to watch himself around Maelstrom, explaining the barber might look like a meek little fellow, but had a firecracker temper that got him arrested for murdering his wife and some traveling salesman he mistakenly took to be her lover.

McDukes waved off the concern.

He shouldn't have, it turns out.

Maelstrom got a gun from one of the guards in trade for a year's worth of haircuts and showed up at McDukes's cell that night. Whether by accident or arrangement, the door wasn't locked. Maelstrom entered, whispered McDukes's name, and fired. The gunshot noise carried throughout the cellblock like a bank of angry thunder.

The bullet caught McDukes below his right shoulder. Ignoring the pain, he leaped from the bunk, tackled Maelstrom, and wrenched the gun from his grip. In the same motion, without hesitation, he turned the weapon on Maelstrom and fired. The bullet cracked teeth sailing into Maelstrom's mouth and out his neck. He was dead before any guards arrived to check out the ruckus.

McDukes was rushed to the prison hospital, and kept for three days of observation against the possibility of infection. His wound was cited in the warden's report as evidence Maelstrom fired first, and he was let off with a reprimand for inspiring a disturbance.

The story that spread among the prisoners grew well out of proportion to the truth, with the best one describing how McDukes, unarmed, had dodged a hail of gunfire before using a toothbrush to bring Maelstrom down. He was treated as a hero his first day back in the courtyard, making his entrance to cheers, handshakes, and back-slaps.

This time Swaney approached McDukes. "You ever consider leaving the cell and moving on?" he said, reprising their earlier conversation.

McDukes cracked an oversized grin. "When I'm ready, Lowell."

"When you're ready, me, too," Swaney said.

With that, they moved to the privacy of the fruit tree bench and discussed a mutual future away from Desert Prison.

Swaney relaxed once McDukes detailed what he had in mind. It was to his liking. They shook hands on the plan and turned their talk from the future to the past days of glory they had shared.

The memories provoked laughter from Swaney, only the barest of smiles from McDukes.

After all, it wasn't as if McDukes intended to let Swaney live much longer.

Swaney had killed his wife.

Swaney had to die.

But not here, not now.

It needed to happen under conditions that served as a fitting tribute to the one and only woman McDukes had never stopped loving.

CHAPTER 2

The tunnel had been dug years ago, when Desert Prison was still a fort, designed as a way for women and their children to escape in the event of an attack by Injuns. It fell into disuse and was eventually forgotten about as civilization encroached on the Wild West.

Ned Buchanan had stumbled across it while prospecting the foothills, made it his secret and his secret alone until he got wind of the misery his old friend McDukes was unable to shake, and offered the tunnel as possibly a better solution to what ailed him than the rotgut whiskey he had made his constant companion.

He was waiting for McDukes and Swaney when they reached the tunnel exit behind a wall of sagebrush about ten miles south of town. He'd spent much of the night there, lacing the area with lye to ward off the search hounds sure to be put on their trail.

Buchanan exchanged warm greetings with McDukes and Swaney before he led them to the mustangs he had saddled and packed with hardtack and other vittles.

Later, when it was safe to slow down for a spell, he cooked them a meal of hot meat and bean soup over an open wood fire.

"Ned, them's quite the fine ponies you got us," McDukes said, making small talk. "I thank you kindly for that."

Buchanan agreed. "Judge a man by the horse under him is what I always say," he said, his wheezing voice thick and deep-throated, like he gargled regularly with iodine. He was as sturdy as McDukes and Swaney, but had a good ten years on them and the surplus of wisdom and knowledge that comes with age. "We reach the ravine I'm aiming us for, there'll be a full storehouse of travel grub, a change of clothing, and an array of weapons," he said.

"Anything you didn't think of?" McDukes said.

Buchanan made a show of eyeing the sky and stroking his gray whiskers. "Anything less than perfect and I wouldn't be yours truly."

Where McDukes applauded the joke, Swaney said, "Sounds like I lost four years behind bars, but you lost no modesty, Mr.

Buchanan."

"Nothing to be modest about, kid."

McDukes said, "He's not fooling, Lowell," backing Buchanan's playfulness. "I got myself sent to prison only because there'd be Ned Buchanan along to backstop me and you escaping."

"And what else, McDukes? What else on your mind was so strong that you were willing to gamble your freedom on Mr. Buchanan being a hundred percent perfect?"

McDukes wasn't about to be trapped into an answer. He rose, dusted himself off, and left their company to wander the desert floor and enjoy the sounds of nighttime creatures crooning discordant melodies under the pale half-moon.

Swaney waited until he was sure McDukes was out of hearing range to ask Buchanan: "Does McDukes still figure to kill me over that wife of his?"

Buchanan wasn't happy about being put on the spot and showed it. "It's his place to say, Swaney, not mine."

"What's your guess then?"

"My guess is best you leave the question alone, same as me. Not knowing is healthy all around and, besides, you're near enough to Hell now you don't need to be stirring the pot any."

23

Swaney left it there.

He didn't sleep well that night, in part because of Buchanan's snoring that cut into the crisp air like the high peep of an oboe. He woke to the smell of fresh coffee and a kettle of hot bean soup laced with beef jerky cooking over the open fire.

McDukes was studying him, sitting at an angle by his saddle pillow, his head leaning against one hand, his elbow propped in the dirt, staring like he had nothing better to do with his time.

He didn't appear angry.

His expression seemed to reflect the strong bond of friendship and trust they had once shared.

At least, that's how Swaney chose to read it, as the look he had come to know the hard way in the earliest days they rode together — beginning with First Refusal.

McDukes's dime novel reputation was already well-known and widespread when Swaney rode into town and confronted him in the First Refusal jailhouse, declaring: "Marshal, I'm here to protect your backside."

"What makes you think I need protecting, mister?"

"Name's Swaney, Lowell Swaney, and

24

protecting is what I been doing to earn my keep, specializing in people who make a habit of stepping into harm's way."

There was something about Swaney that appealed to McDukes, especially his swagger and the way he spoke with the confidence of a cowpoke adept at putting living way out in front of losing, same as him.

"I get two hundred in silver every month," McDukes said. "You willing to come in for twenty of that, I'll give you a trial run."

"Your friendship is payment enough until I prove my worth to your satisfaction, Marshal."

"Friendship is a word I don't use lightly, Swaney."

"Makes it worth more than twenty pieces of silver to my way of thinking."

Without another word, McDukes fished a deputy's badge from a desk drawer and tossed it to Swaney, who snatched it from the air in seconds. "Hope you're that fast with your shooter," McDukes said.

"Faster, whenever it matters."

Swaney proved his brag in the months that followed, helping enforce McDukes's edict that no guns were permitted inside the town boundaries. One early incident the popular dime novelist Ned Buntline came to write about involved the notorious hell-raiser

Stamps Berland, who arrived in First Refusal intending to tarnish McDukes's reputation and win notoriety for himself.

He was a foot taller than McDukes.

All muscle on a fearsome frame.

A maniacal look in his heavy-lidded eyes.

Definitely not someone to be taken for granted or tampered with.

Berland parked himself at the First National Saloon of First Refusal, kept one Frontier Target holstered, and slapped the other pistol on the bar top. He yelled for bourbon — *the real stuff and leave the bottle* — and shouted a challenge to McDukes or anyone else dumb enough to try relieving him of his weapons, and waited for McDukes to show his face.

Tommy Hodges, age eight and later famous as the territory's first U.S. senator, there to collect a bucket of beer for his mom and pop back home, went racing after McDukes with the news.

McDukes slapped on his twin Frontiers and headed for the saloon, cruised through the swinging doors, and, calm as a cucumber, inquired: "Which one of you's the loudmouth who believes himself larger than the law?"

"That would be me, you pissant," Berland said, displaying his Frontier Target.

26

The room grew quieter than a grave.

Everyone froze in anticipation of what might happen next.

They didn't have long to wait.

McDukes wasted no steps marching over to Berland and answering Berland's stare with one of his own before he grabbed the Frontier Target from the bar top and used it to crack Berland over the head. Berland crashed to the floor, tipping a spittoon, whose gunk washed over his face.

"Anytime you think to break the rules, I'll be around to break your skull, mister. You understand?"

McDukes stepped back as Berland pulled himself back onto his boots. "Understood," he said, but it was a ruse that gave him the few seconds more he needed to shake his head clear and whip out his holstered pistol.

He had it aimed at McDukes before McDukes could draw, slowed down by the surprise of Berland's swift recovery.

"You're a dead man, McDukes! Get ready to meet your maker!"

Bang!

Only Berland hadn't fired the shot that caught him in his shooting arm, causing him to drop his weapon.

It was Swaney. He had slipped into the bar without notice and posted himself across the room behind McDukes.

Bang!

The second shot dropped Berland to the floor again, this time permanently.

Swaney holstered his Colt and called to McDukes, "You okay, Marshal?"

"Better'n him, deputy. Thanks."

"No thanks necessary. Was only doing my job."

The story Ned Buntline came to write played up Swaney's part in the incident, along with manufacturing a history of heroics that made him out to be the equal of McDukes in what led to further stories marking the adventures of Swaney and McDukes as often as they marked the adventures of McDukes and Swaney.

McDukes laughed it off.

Swaney treated it for the truth.

So did James Butler Hickok, pausing on a pass through First Refusal to rest his pony and pay his respects to McDukes. They were old friends, had shared an adventure or two when they were younger.

Tommy Hodges was there to bail out his father when Hickok strutted into the marshal's office bigger than life, catching McDukes by surprise before they shared a warm embrace and words of mutual admiration. Tommy grew nervous at the thought of meeting the great "Wild Bill," so much so that, when Hickok invited a handshake, the tyke held out his hand and stuttered: "Glad t-t-to meet you, Mr. Hiccup."

Laughter filled the room, none louder than from Swaney, who Wild Bill recognized from illustrations accompanying Ned Buntline's prose, a primary source of the reputation enjoyed by Hickok.

"Your body count seems to rise with every new edition," Hickok said.

"Never hope to rise to your exalted level, Wild Bill."

"Be glad. With every Beadle Weekly or Buntline tale comes some varmint out of the brush looking to take me on and secure his own reputation."

"You try talking them out of such foolishness?"

"Waste of good air. I wish them Godspeed and shoot to kill. They die and I move on, knowing there'll be a next time. There's always a next time. Good thing I like to kill, but you shouldn't follow my lead, Swaney. Better you should take your lead from McDukes. Turn the other cheek long and hard as you can, unless killing is also to your taste."

Swaney said, "I'll take that advice as my golden rule, seeing as how it comes from you, Bill."

Hickok nodded approval and turned his attention to McDukes.

"You got a good man here, McDukes. If you're in need, you got yourself a good man guarding your backside."

"Thanks for telling me what I already know, Bill."

"No charge for the service, old bud, and now I gotta find me a tub and a shave and some busty wench to curb my appetite for companionship before settling at some honest card table for a spell."

"After parking your twin shooters here with me first, for safekeeping."

"I'd feel safer keeping them cinched to my thighs, but if that's your rule I'm not one to disrespect it." He undid his gun belt, handed it over, and marched off.

McDukes said, "That's a man to admire, Swaney. Somebody out to get his name in the history books might come along some day and somehow kill him, but no way is Wild Bill ever dying."

Buchanan came hustling up to the campfire.

"I sense a prison posse coming for us in the distance and getting closer by the minute," Buchanan said, hustling up to the campfire. "Time to saddle and git. Time's still not on our side."

Swaney and McDukes knew by now to trust Buchanan's instincts.

Swaney dumped what was left of the soup and coffee. McDukes packed their soogans and lashed them to the mustangs. Buchanan obliterated all traces of the campsite.

They were ready just shy of ten minutes later to gallop off, putting the rising orange sun at their backs.

McDukes mounted, saying, "I hope you won't have us hurrying like this through our next stop, Ned. Not even you could be that cruel and deny us the merriment we been talking about."

"I could be and I will be comes to that, McDukes. You got me involved to escape you and Swaney free and clear from Desert Prison. I ain't letting nothing slow us down or put a halt to that objective, certainly not no stinking women."

Swaney said, "Aw, Ned, it's been four years since I had anything but a fruit tree to wrap my legs around."

"No easier way to lose a chase than over some woman of pleasure, Swaney, especially when the pot you're playing for is your freedom," Buchanan said, and took off.

He couldn't know at the time that Swaney and McDukes would shortly encounter a woman named Jeanne d'Evreaux, who'd stir a conflict between them as great as the conflict caused by the death of McDukes's wife, already boiling below the surface.

It wasn't the posse on their tail, after all.

At closer range, it appeared to be a lone rider raising dust on the trail.

Buchanan, never one to take unnecessary chances, called for Swaney and McDukes to drop from sight and be ready for the worst while he continued riding the road as a distraction.

Swaney chose an elevated spot fifty yards away, safe from discovery, but with a good view of the road for himself.

McDukes decided on a hiding place behind a tall clump of bushes, but didn't get there quick enough to avoid being seen by the lone rider, name of Trouble Lamonica, who like his brother, Evil, was a bounty hunter growing rich on reward money.

"That you, McDukes?" Lamonica called out, motioning with his double-barrel shotgun. "C'mon and make yourself known. The name's Trouble Lamonica and I got me a sweet payday waiting at Desert Prison, fifty gold smackers, when I bring you back dead or alive, the former if you're foolish enough to make it a contest with me."

McDukes stepped out onto the trail.

Not in surrender.

In fairness.

He couldn't take Trouble Lamonica down without giving him a fair shake at turning back empty-handed and told him so.

"Your reputation, it don't scare me none. I already got you in my sights and can squeeze both triggers before you draw your iron, McDukes."

There's something about a shotgun that makes stupid men brave, not wise.

McDukes sighed, whipped out his side-arm, and sent Lamonica to meet his maker with a neat hole between his bushy eyebrows.

Within the hour, he, Swaney, and Buchanan had buried Lamonica by the side of the road, marked his grave with a makeshift cross and a mound of rocks, and resumed their journey, taking the bounty hunter's horse in payment for the effort.

A search of Lamonica's saddlebags produced paperwork with his Christian name — it was "Christian" — and showed a family address in Bangor, Maine. Later, when there was time and opportunity, McDukes posted a letter to them describing how Christian had lost his life to a renegade band of Injuns in a brave defense of six

33

orphaned youths and three desperate widows. He signed it "Wyatt Earp, U.S. Marshal."

Swaney chided him over that. "I don't hardly know how Earp would take to your using his name in that fashion," he said.

McDukes said, "He's welcome to sign my name as payback, he chooses," and that ended the discussion.

Lamonica's saddlebags also contained a modest amount of gold and a land deed to some far west acres in a place called Tap Dance.

Buchanan flipped one of the dead man's coins in a winner's choice won by McDukes.

He chose the gold.

Swaney got the land.

Buchanan said, "Congratulations, Swaney. I guess that makes you a land baron." He showed him on his map where Tap Dance was located. "You get to the *ciudad* of angels, Los Angeles herself out California way, you've gone too far," he said.

Swaney said, "I'm up for the ride."

McDukes said, "Good a place as any to aim for."

Buchanan said, "Then Tap Dance it is, gents."

And off they rode.

CHAPTER 3

The town of First Refusal, on the route to Tap Dance, was not much more than a prairie stop for weary drovers and wandering cowpokes, with a modest resident population under one hundred. It consisted of a general store, a seedy hotel, a stable, a saloon, and Ma Rooney's whorehouse, where Buchanan directed Swaney and McDukes to, once they freshened up at the hotel.

Swaney used the opportunity to shave off his mustache and beard, exposing high cheeks and a square jaw, turning him into somebody who could pass for a stranger even among old friends.

McDukes, on the other hand, made his heavy crop of straw-colored whiskers into a sleek goatee and let it go at that, counting on his blue eyes to project a sense of innocence and safety to anyone studying him for familiarity.

Buchanan had touted Ma Rooney to their coming before he wandered off to the saloon. She greeted them warmly, like favored customers, and spoke highly of Buchanan as someone who knew her back when, "back when" being before her figure doubled in size and her face became a haven for crow's feet, wrinkles, and sagging skin.

With that, she trotted out her seven best girls for their inspection and told them in a voice that sparkled like champagne, "No charge, boys. You leave my establishment happy as a June bug, I expect you'll tell friends about the good times to be had at Ma Rooney's and be coming back yourselves."

Six of the seven whores looked like they'd been chewed on once too often.

The exception was the whore calling herself Jeanne d'Evreaux.

McDukes would say years later, "In all my life, Jeanne was the most beautiful. In all my eternity, too, probably."

It may have been Swaney said it.

In any event, it was said and it was heard.

That part is the truth.

And both men coveted her.

That part is also the truth.

Jeanne's face inspired the challenge, starting with exotic eyes enhanced by long, erotic lashes that signaled danger with every blink. Her majestic nose was straight with a modest tip to the end. Her full lower jaw led to a dimpled chin. Bangs brushed back from her strong forehead and straight, silken brown hair cascaded down past her broad, bare shoulders. She had youth on her side, too, with all the insinuating, coquettish allure that marks a beauty not yet turned twenty.

Swaney won a coin toss and headed upstairs to gambol with Jeanne.

Afterward, glowing with something greater than satisfaction, he headed down along the squeaky boardwalk to join Buchanan at the saloon while McDukes tramped upstairs to take his turn with Jeanne.

Stepping through the swinging doors onto the sawdust, Swaney understood the unusual silence when he saw Buchanan stretched out on an empty poker table, sleeping or worse, a gambler holding him in place with a Bowie knife lodged against his throat.

Kerosene lamps gave an eerie luster to the scene, like some tableau on a picture postcard or inside on the pages of *The National Police Gazette*.

"That's not polite, mister," Swaney shouted at him from across the room. "I urge you to step away from my good friend Mr. Buchanan, and we can talk a saner way to settle your beef."

"Too late, mister. My mind is fixed on his getting what he deserves from me."

"Then you'll also have to deal me in," Swaney said, and moved his shooting hand toward his holster.

The gambler, neither dissuaded nor intimidated, answered by pitching his Bowie at him. The blade whizzed past Swaney by inches and continued out through the swinging doors into the muddy darkness.

Swaney fired, his reflexes keen as ever. The years behind prison walls had not slowed him down any. The gambler was dead before he hit the floor.

Cowhands and bar regulars crowded around Swaney, congratulating him while he roused Buchanan from his drunken sleep by showering him with tankards of beer and administering a string of hard slaps before dragging him to their horses parked behind Ma Rooney's place.

There was a sudden urgency to leaving town.

He had been recognized.

He had heard his name shifting in whispers from one pair of lips to another.

Word was bound to carry back to the

38

posse chasing after him.

Worse, there could have been drifters in the room who knew about the reward money on his head and might be foolish enough to make a play.

Swaney strapped Buchanan to his horse and rushed inside the whorehouse, anxious to induct McDukes into this new state of affairs and get back on the trail to Tap Dance.

McDukes was feeling guilt and shame before Swaney burst into the room, out of breath, shouting for him to get dressed and hurry up about it. Jeanne d'Evreaux was the first woman he had been with since the death of his wife and he'd felt compelled to tell her that.

"Flattered, I am," she said, softly, studying his crystal-clear features and pushing aside some of the long blond strands that fell over his ear and running a finger over his mustache, making small circles on his chest. "Do you have some regret, *mon ami*?"

"I should, I reckon, but I don't. You? Have you slept with many men since settling in at Ma Rooney's?"

"I've been to bed with many men, *oui,* yes, dozens, but never to sleep. Bed is for the men I have to be with. Sleep is for the men

39

I want to be with." Her voice carried the melody of bright winds through whistling reeds, while the French accent added a lyric of love.

"Where do I rank?"

She ignored his question for one of her own. "Tell me about her, your wife who you so clearly loved and love still — I see it in your eyes — will you?"

McDukes had never talked about Ellie's death with anyone, but he was tempted now, by the emotion building inside him for Jeanne d'Evreaux's favor, wondering if that's what it would take for her to choose sleep over bed with him. Wondering, how to explain why he had vowed vengeance against Swaney. Wondering most of all what would Ellie think, how she would feel about him staining bed sheets with someone else. He felt himself near tears as he wrestled with the problem.

Swaney's arrival saved him from a decision.

"Back into your britches, cowboy," he said. "With all due apologies to the beautiful lady by your side, we got an urgent need to hotfoot it out of town."

Swaney told Ma Rooney they were leaving the spare horse to her, the one that had belonged to Trouble Lamonica, with their compliments. She thanked both with a hug and a handshake, asked them to *"Tell that damn old rogue Buchanan to be careful Demon Rum don't drive him to no early grave,"* and got back to business, sending one of her regular customers, Cactus Billy Clemens, upstairs.

"It's me again, dearest Jeanne, your Billy Boy," he said, parking his ten gallon and holster on the door hook. He tossed away his sweat-stained bandana, unbuttoned his shirt, and dropped his trousers.

Jeanne d'Evreaux finished remaking the bed and patted for him to take his usual place, anxious to make Cactus Billy comfortable.

He was nice.

She liked him.

He was a kid, a year or two younger than she, but he had an easy way about him, and treated her with kindness and respect frequently lacking in the smelly old men two and three times his age, who behaved like they owned her outright.

Afterward, holding her in his arms, Cactus Billy said, "You know I'd marry you this very minute, you give me the sign, sweet Jeanne. Whaddaya say?"

"You deserve better than me, *mon ami.*"

"You're always telling me that, but it's you that I want."

She silenced him with a lingering kiss, the best answer he ever got from her, for all the times he raised the question, so he was neither discouraged nor dismayed.

Some months later, Jeanne d'Evreaux's mood swings became more impetuous and her habits matched cycles with the moon. She fainted more than once. Her corset became tougher to cinch, then impossible. Her complexion turned the rich color of fresh cream.

Ma Rooney could no longer stay silent. "Tell me, Jeanne. Who was he? Which one done it to you?"

Jeanne caved to the truth. *"Je ne sais pas."*

"English, dammit."

"I don't know, Ma."

"Don't know or ain't tellin', which is it?"

"Je ne sais pas. I don't know."

"Goin' by my calendar and reckoning, how's McDukes for a winning guess?"

Jeanne hunched her shoulders and shrugged.

"Swaney, then. Was it Swaney aimed you for motherhood?"

"Or maybe even Cactus Billy," Jeanne said, stone-faced.

CHAPTER 4

There were two attempts on the lives of Swaney and McDukes before they reached New Testament, the next stop on the Minute Grande route to Tap Dance mapped out by Buchanan. The first was by Evil Lamonica, chasing after the same reward money that had cost his brother, Trouble, his life. He came upon them with the quiet stealth equal to a wily Injun, catching them unawares.

"Drop your hardware before I drop you," he said, brandishing his powerful, custom-made Philippine. Its large trigger guard and long trigger allowed him to get off shots quickly, without removing his patent leather gloves.

McDukes, Swaney, and Buchanan obliged Lamonica.

Knowing the wanted posters specified "dead or alive," he announced "dead" best suited his style and offered them a ten-

43

count showdown on the desert turf. "Don't care who tries me first," he said. McDukes and Swaney stepped forward in unison.

"You," Lamonica said, pointing at McDukes, and instructed Buchanan to mark the field of play. "You'll also do the count-off to ten, mister, if'n for a fact you know how to reach that high with your numbers."

Buchanan grumbled a response.

"Doesn't matter if he does or don't," Swaney said. "You won't be around to hear." He dropped to the ground, got hold of his Colt, and fired before the bounty hunter's reflexes could respond.

That was the end of Evil Lamonica.

Like his brother before him, Evil was carrying a fair measure of currency and paperwork, putting his acreage in Top Dance adjacent to what had been Trouble's parcels and now belonged to Swaney.

A coin toss again decided who got what.

Swaney won and added to his land holdings.

McDukes added to his gold coins and folding money.

Both invited Buchanan to take the dead man's pinto for his own, and that was that until time and circumstance permitted McDukes to scratch out a letter of condolence and send it to Lamonica's wife in Newark, New Jersey. Instead of "Wyatt Earp, U.S. Marshal" as on the missive to his brother Trouble's survivors in Bangor, Maine, McDukes signed this one "William F. Cody, Famous Buffalo Hunter."

George Tatum was the other bounty hunter intent on profiting off Swaney and McDukes. He was less skilled than either Lamonica brother, a tenderfoot from the east who'd spent a dime too many buying into magazine tales of fearlessness and dreamed of Buntline stories that might paint him as a hero. He had devoted hours to practicing with a six-iron until convinced he was equal to the best of the bad men.

The tenderfoot somehow found their campsite and sneaked in under cover of darkness. Swaney, McDukes, and Buchanan were asleep after a hard day on the trail under the unrelenting heat of a desert sun that had climbed to over a hundred degrees.

Inching up on McDukes, his weapon drawn, the tenderfoot stumbled over a rock.

McDukes's heavy snore kept him from hearing the noise.

Not so Swaney. He recognized danger when he heard it. He drew his six-shooter from under his saddle, used his ears to compass where the sound came from, and blasted away.

The bullets smashed into Tatum and sent him reeling backward on his boot heels before he dropped, already too dead to care about the blood pouring from him.

Swaney checked his handiwork.

Satisfied, he got back to bed and returned to his dreams.

Neither McDukes nor Buchanan had stirred. It wasn't until sunrise that they realized there had been an intruder. They buried him without fanfare except for a grave marker made from discarded wagon wood on which Buchanan used his gutting blade to carve "Tatum/Late Him" and the date.

McDukes resented that Tatum appeared ready to kill him in his sleep. He called it a cowardly act. He insisted that the man's belongings, including his weapons and his saddle, be buried with him, and thought to add: "There'll be no letter to his family from me, that's for certain."

"I'll kill his horse, that makes you any happier," Swaney said.

"No, sir," Buchanan said. "You'll have to get by me first."

"As easy done as said, Ned."

McDukes quieted their simmering war of

words before it got out of hand. "Turn the animal loose to the wilds, and that'll satisfy me," he said.

Later, back on the trail, during a pause to fill their canteens from a clear water stream, McDukes thought to thank Swaney for again saving his life.

It was the opening Swaney was waiting for to raise the delicate issue of Ellie McDukes.

He said, "About your wife, McDukes. About Ellie. You still blame me?"

"Damn right I do."

"You're still wrong then."

"No difference."

"To me a difference."

"To you," McDukes agreed.

Swaney, struggling to maintain his calm and seeming indifference, said, "I suppose it stays your plan to kill me?"

"Where before I wouldn't go to the trouble, for now I owe you at least that much an answer. Yes, indeed I do."

He left Swaney, climbed back on his horse, and galloped off, passing Buchanan, who was taking a dump in the brush. Buchanan pulled up his britches, moseyed over to Swaney, and said, "What did I miss?"

Swaney repeated the conversation.

Buchanan said, "You ask me, maybe it's

time for you to set off on your own instead of hanging around for a showdown that, knowing McDukes as I do, is sure as eggs to come."

"I don't think so, Ned. I figure there's still time for that ill-tempered partner of mine to come to his senses. Besides, it's the crazy people what run from danger. It's the sane people what know to keep danger in their sights."

Buchanan got around to privately sharing Swaney's exchange with McDukes before they reached New Testament.

McDukes was amused. "I owe what I owe, not what other people decide," he said. "I got my own plans for Lowell Swaney. That's all keeping him alive for now. That and only that, Ned. Nothing else. Only that."

48

CHAPTER 5

New Testament was safe harbor for every fetcher, shootist, thief, thug, fakir, mouth, militant, and bunko-artist on the run from the law. Even the Pinkertons respected the town boundaries and steered clear, figuring a lawbreaker deserved someplace safe, where he could reevaluate his life and maybe choose to take the glory road to an honest, God-fearing future.

Any disputes that might arise by law had to be settled outside the town boundaries that ran a mile in every direction from the rusted, dry-well pump in the center of New Testament Square. The punishment for infraction was a swift and certain death. No ceremony was made of it. The township *padrones* were more anxious to accentuate positive values than offenses to the spirit of love and forgiveness.

An instigator, whether male or female, was led to the pens, stripped of clothing, and

49

fed live to the pigs.

It occurred fewer than eight times in any given year.

Swaney and McDukes learned this from Buchanan as they passed into New Testament through the main entrance gate. Buchanan was well-known here, well-respected, even tolerated by the *padrones,* who often elected to ignore his losing battles with whiskey, carried on the book of rules and regulations as cause for instant banishment. No one remembered exactly why that wasn't the case with Buchanan, but figured it was repayment for some distant act of heroism. Buchanan never let on he knew better.

McDukes said, "How long we staying here, Ned?"

Buchanan said, "A week minimum, a month most, I reckon, before I figure for certain the posse has given up the chase and ain't no longer out there."

They bathed, shaved, and treated themselves to an expensive meal of steak and trimmings at China Loo's place before Buchanan wandered off to settle on a bar stool at the Golden Spade Saloon, a short stroll down from their hotel.

Swaney was up for an evening between the sheets.

So was McDukes, surprised the urge had grown since they left First Refusal, maybe, he considered, to test his true feelings about Jeanne d'Evreaux.

There were two whorehouses to choose from, Madam Fanny's and Madam Annie's. They were sisters. Once partners, they had quarreled — over what was their secret — and gone their separate ways. Fanny took the building, the furnishings, and half the whores. Annie took the rest of the whores and moved into a failed two-story bank building across the road.

A flip of a coin sent Swaney to Madam Fanny's and McDukes to Madam Annie's.

"We can share our findings later or maybe even trade places for the fun of it," Swaney said. "How's that idea sit with you, McDukes?"

"Vulgar," McDukes said, and headed to Madam Annie's, where a surprise awaited him when the madam, a crusty old bird with crafty eyes and bad teeth stained yellow from too much chewing tobacco, trotted out her inventory, had them line up, and vouched for their skills and cleanliness.

Jeanne d'Evreaux was among them.

She seemed on the edge of collapse when she realized it was McDukes staring back at her with a stunned expression, shaking his

51

head in disbelief.

He pulled himself together, walked over, and grabbed her by the wrist. "This one will do me fine," he said, and Jeanne led him to her room on the second floor.

At first they made love in passionate silence.

Then they made love in noisy heat and anger.

Finally, exhausted, they stared at one another in silence until McDukes said, "Tell me everything I should know."

"It may not make you happy, *mon amour.*"

"Tell me anyway."

She had arrived in New Testament not so many weeks ago, with Cactus Billy Clemens. Their intention was to marry, save the child she was carrying from the stigma of going through life as a fatherless bastard.

There was no certainty Cactus Billy was the father.

She told him so.

He didn't care.

He said, "The child must have a name and I'm pleased to give him mine, so long as you come with the bargain, beautiful Jeanne."

Ma Rooney helped Jeanne pack her meager belongings and, after Cactus Billy paid her the two-hundred-dollar dowry she had demanded, gave Jeanne a warm kiss good-bye and helped her into Cactus Billy's buckboard, telling him, "The money has only bought you this fine girl, Billy. I'm throwing in the child at no extra cost. Treat them with kindness, you know what's good for you, or I'll come a-hunting."

Cactus Billy's folks were not as under-standing. They were an old-fashioned couple who knew the Bible word for word and never missed a prayer at the dinner table or a Sunday church service.

"Any horse's tail can catch cockleburs," his father said before disinheriting Cactus Billy and ordering: "Don't you or your whore woman come around here ever again, you know what's good for you."

His mother, weeping like prairie rain, called after her only son and his bride-to-be as they headed off in the buckboard, "Write, but remember not to visit."

Cactus Billy was a superior cactus-drainer, but there was little business to be found in New Testament, where two other cactus-drainers had developed a thriving business. He was reluctant to marry Jeanne without a steady income.

They agreed she should take up the work she knew well while he went looking for a town that needed a cactus-drainer with his superior skills. He guessed it would be a few weeks, maybe a month, before he returned with good news, and off he went.

Madam Annie didn't hesitate to take Jeanne on upon hearing she was fresh from First Refusal and Ma Rooney's keep and care. "That woman has never suffered a sour apple, so I'm glad to welcome you," she said. "The pay ain't much more'n chicken feed, but any tips you get are yours to keep a hunnert percent."

Jeanne compulsively touched McDukes on the cheek, blew out a sigh of relief, and forced a smile. "So now you know, *mon amour.* If you choose to leave me, race away and disappear from my life. I will be sad, but I will understand."

"Shame on you," McDukes said. "You believe I'd do that, your head is as thick as your belly's getting." He took hold of her hands. "Fate decreed I was meant to find you again. I got no intention of losing you now or ever."

"But there's Billy —"

"You two ain't hitched yet?"

"No."

"And the baby? You said you don't know for a fact it's his?"

"I don't."

"So I could be the father?"

"Yes."

"Or Lowell Swaney could be the father?"

"Yes."

"Who else?"

"I don't keep a list, *mon amour.*"

"Doesn't matter."

"I need to prove how much I love you."

"Don't need proof, but —"

She was on top of him, smothering him with hungry kisses before McDukes could finish the thought.

Finally worn out, they fell into a deep sleep.

She was still sleeping when he snapped awake about an hour later and put his mind to remembering the scheme that had come to him as a dream, superior to any plan he'd been storing in his thoughts.

He shook her gently to get her attention. "I got some important business needs caring for, honey pot, but I'll be back to get you right after that, so you be ready to git," he said.

"Whatever you say, *mon amour.*"

McDukes left her to put into play the next move in his new plan to avenge the death of his dear, precious Ellie by ridding the world of Lowell Swaney.

■ ■ ■

Over breakfast at China Loo's, Swaney finished describing in extravagant detail how well-spent his time was at Madam Fanny's, first with one whore, then another. And another. "Even learning some new tricks before I was worn down to the bone and near passed out in the saddle, McDukes. First time that ever happened."

McDukes fed him some false sympathy and waited for Swaney to inquire about his own evening at Madam Annie's, certain it was coming, given Swaney's penchant for that kind of tell-all talk.

He put on a glum look to advance Swaney's curiosity.

It came soon enough.

"You look none too happy, making me surmise your time in the playground was less a success than mine, not that I figure it could match or exceed what I just told you," Swaney said.

"It's news I'm not pleased to share with you, Swaney."

"All the better. Let's hear it."

McDukes held back a bit longer before giving in to Swaney's insistent urging.

"Jeanne," he said. "Jeanne d'Evreaux."

"Jeanne?" Swaney eased upright in his chair and eyed McDukes with curiosity. "What about her?"

"I mentioned your name and she began wailing for all get-out, saying you're the father of the unborn child she's now carrying in her womb."

Swaney was stunned by the news. "What else?"

"You remember Cactus Billy Clemens? Was him who claimed the baby for his own, only to run away with her and turn her over to Madam Annie. He takes every penny she earns."

"You dick her getting at the facts? I need to know, McDukes?"

"It was on my mind, but not after I learned her situation, saw her break up longing for you, and heard her calling the child to come by the name she's already pinned on him: Lowell Swaney, Jr."

Lies, of course, but so what, McDukes told himself.

Swaney was buying it as the truth.

That's what mattered.

Swaney gripped his coffee mug and pitched it across the dining room, shattering the oversized pewter-framed wall mirror behind China Loo's counter. "Gonna find and kill that sumbitch Cactus Billy Clemens for what he done to that precious girl of mine," he said, pushing up from the table.

McDukes said, "Slow it down, Lowell." He grabbed Swaney by the wrist. "Maybe you should first visit Jeanne, let her know you intend getting her away from Cactus Billy?"

"Already had that same good idea, McDukes. Where I'll be heading right now."

McDukes gave it five minutes before leaving China Loo's to look for Cactus Billy.

He found him at the blacksmith's, waiting for the smithy to fit his horse for new shoes.

"I don't believe in ever spilling beans, Billy, but you need to know that my partner, Swaney, is heading on over to Madam Annie's as I speak, planning to kill your bride-to-be, Jeanne."

"This some kind of joke, McDukes?"

"Wish it were, Billy, for your sake, but I know Swaney good enough to know when he's saying what he means, like now."

"He say why?"

"For deceiving him the way she run off with you after promising herself to him back in First Refusal, something like that, and how he'll be gunning for you next, for carrying on about how you're falsely claiming his unborn child as your own."

58

Cactus Billy took the news calmly. He called to the smithy, "Hank, I'll be gone for a bit. Some personal business needs my immediate attention."

McDukes said, "Billy, you're carrying a Smith & Wesson, but you ain't no gunslinger. You don't stand a chance in Hell taking on Swaney by yourself, if that's your intent. Let me go with you to Madam Annie's, a practiced hand to back your play."

"Thank you kindly, McDukes, but this is something, come what may, I need do for myself. Jeanne needs protecting, I'm the man to give it to her, or what kind of husband and father could I ever make myself out to be?"

Swaney was gone from Madam Annie's before Cactus Billy got there.

So was Jeanne.

As the madam explained in the complaint lodged with the *padrones* and afterward widely reported in dime novels, she tried turning Swaney away after he announced he had come to take Jeanne to a better life.

She said, "I don't know you from Adam, mister, but, you don't make yourself scarce, I'll be screaming bloody shit for help from the *padrones,* and you know what that gets you — a quick one-way trip to the pig pens."

Swaney pulled out his Colt and pressed the barrel between her ample bosoms. "Damn the *padrones* and their rules," he said. "This says you're gonna call for Jeanne to dress herself decent and come on here to you, unless you're anxious to meet your maker."

"I saw in that critter's eyes he had no intention of leaving without her and was ready to make good on his threat," Madam Annie said. "I did what I was told, and it could not-a been more'n ten minutes before Jeanne showed her pretty face, looking nervous and a little surprised."

"You are not who I expected," Jeanne said.

She turned, planning to return to her room.

Swaney ordered her to stop.

Jeanne ignored his command.

He grabbed onto her and apologized before landing a hard blow to the chin that knocked her out; then hoisted her featherweight frame over his shoulder and left, ignoring the curses Madam Annie was throwing at him. "Damn your hide! You're a dead man by your own doing," she said. "You hear me, mister? You listening good?"

Swaney carted Jeanne to the livery stable, racing to quit town before the madam turned the *padrones* on him. He stumbled into Ned Buchanan stretched out on a bed of bundled hay, sleeping off his latest bar-room binge at the Golden Spade, smelling like he had consumed an entire brewery.

One hard kick and Buchanan was awake, rubbing the sleep from his eyes and trying to decipher why Swaney was carting Jeanne like that. "I sense you been up to no good, Lowell," was the best he could come up with.

Swaney spilled out the circumstances in precise detail.

Buchanan raised his head to the heavens, disturbed by what he heard. "You are instant pig-swill for certain, the *padrones* catch you," he said. "Get her on the pinto and follow my lead, out past the town boundaries to a hiding spot I know from history, swell enough until I can think better."

"You sure you want to put yourself in danger by this act of generosity, Ned?"

Buchanan said, "No child should grow up without a father, so make like there's a burr in your britches and saddle up. We got no time to waste."

Buchanan was back in town an hour or so later.

61

He headed his mustang straight for the Golden Spade to celebrate how Swaney's escape with Jeanne went without incident.

Settling on a bar stool, he spotted McDukes and Cactus Billy Clemens sharing a table left and center of the swinging doors. Cactus Billy was well into his cups, wailing something fierce within earshot of all, about that dirty dog Lowell Swaney having kidnapped his wife and unborn child, trying to claim them for his own.

McDukes, sober, his drink barely touched, was encouraging Cactus Billy in his misery.

"Was me, I wouldn't be pinning my hopes on the *padrones* catching up to Swaney and turning him into pig feed anytime soon, if at all, not for all the tea in China," he said. "Seeing how Swaney didn't think twice about stealing Jeanne out from under you, I'd want to invest in someone who can return her to your loving arms faster and more certain than that, Billy."

"You talking about yourself, McDukes?"

"Would if I could, Billy boy, but I got my own situation to worry about, keeping ahead of a posse after me for busting Swaney out of prison, wrong as can be in thinking he deserved his freedom." He made a show of studying the room. "Over there, Billy, see — Juan Forminfante and

Denny Slime. Always up for hire. One or both might agree to take on Swaney and return Jeanne to you unharmed."

Cactus Billy excused himself, crossed the room, joined Juan Forminfante and Denny Slime at their table, and proceeded to engage them in whispered conversation that concluded with Cactus Billy counting out a pile of folding money and the three men trading handshakes.

He hadn't noticed what Buchanan saw for certain — Forminfante sending a sly smile and a hurried two-finger salute of thanks at McDukes from the brim of his four-creased topper.

The gesture confirmed what Buchanan was thinking — McDukes was double-dealing from the bottom of the deck, setting in motion two ways from Sunday how Swaney could go to his final reward.

McDukes was finally getting even about Ellie without dirtying his own hands, the same way Ellie came to be killed by the Kangaroo Kid and Arapaho Morgan while on the run from a posse closing in on Swaney. At least, Buchanan figured, that's what McDukes had reckoned all this time and why vengeance was writ large in his craw.

What galled Buchanan most was being

dragged unwittingly into McDukes's scheme, first by making it possible for him to spring Swaney from Desert Prison, next by setting into motion a situation in New Testament that sent the *padrones* after Swaney.

Had McDukes been honest about his motive to begin with, Buchanan would have refused to have anything to do with him.

His long friendship with McDukes no longer held any appeal.

It was over and done with, finished for good.

He drank to his resolve and was still drinking hard when McDukes settled alongside him, after Cactus Billy left with Forminfante and Denny Slime.

"Time for you and me to saddle up and leave this town behind us, Ned."

"What about Swaney?"

"He ain't coming, Ned. Lowell's found more to occupy his time in New Testament than interests me."

"What about Tap Dance and his land holdings there?"

"I asked him and he said no rush, the land would still be there when he got around to it."

McDukes, damn him, still lying through his teeth.

Buchanan fought the urge to slam McDukes in the face with the truth.

For what reason?

To earn an apology?

To inspire a new lie was the more likely outcome.

Buchanan figured he was entitled to a lie of his own. "You got the map, so go on and travel alone, McDukes. I still got private matters holding me here."

"Then serve yourself, old friend. I'll leave you behind, knowing we'll be painting the same trail together sometime later, somewhere downwind."

Buchanan thought, *Not if I can help it,* and shortly set off by himself on a little used trail, intending to lead Swaney and Jeanne to safety away from the *padrones* and Cactus Billy's hired guns, Forminfante and Denny Slime.

They weren't where he'd had them hide out.

No trace of them anywhere.

McDukes was three days gone from New Testament, wondering once more about the status of Swaney and Jeanne d'Evreaux, wondering if Swaney was dead by now, wondering if Cactus Billy was caring for Jeanne, unaware it was only until he could

65

return, reclaim her as his own, and give their child his name, when a roving band of outlaws called "Skunkers" took him prisoner.

They caught him by surprise, while he was taking a wash in a modest stream a few yards off the road, or he would have grabbed his Colt and Winchester and dropped all eight before they managed a shot. It wouldn't have been the first time he was outmanned and outgunned but beat the odds.

The Skunkers lashed him to a tree, chose the branch of a knotty pine, and used it to beat McDukes to a bloody pulp. Not yet satisfied, they staked him naked to the ground and poured molasses over him to attract ants and other insects. Then they left him burning under a hot sun that after four days without water or sustenance pushed him to the brink of death.

How he managed to survive the ordeal would come to be told in many different versions in the dime novels. Most of the stories played to his heroic status, gave him sole credit for freeing himself, and left readers to decide for themselves. McDukes subscribed to whatever explanation was put before him when, sadly, he had no knowledge of the truth.

The many blows to the head levied by the Skunkers had cost him his memory.

McDukes remembered nothing.

Another day, it might have been his mind altogether that snapped.

It's best to believe he was rescued by an Injun girl, who stumbled upon him, struggled to get him to the safety of her cabin hideout in the hills, tended to his wounds, nursed him back to health, and, in a trick of fate, back to a reunion with Lowell Swaney.

But first Swaney had to lose his way.

And then Jeanne d'Evreaux.

CHAPTER 6

Swaney and Jeanne had accidentally strayed from Ned Buchanan's map. They ranked it a calamity easy to correct until their mounts balked beyond control when winds of hurricane force swept across the desert floor and sent them searching for safety before the storm might somehow harm their unborn child.

By this time, Jeanne had accepted Swaney's explanation of past events, how both Cactus Billy and he had been misrepresented to her by McDukes. The idea McDukes would give her up so easily bothered her, but she believed it was in her own best interest to accept Swaney as her lover, protector, and husband-to-be, at least for now. She took to calling Swaney *mon amour,* but it was always McDukes she pictured.

They had found shelter in a cave carved out of the rugged hillside and were locked in an intimate embrace, trading promises of eternal love, when a traveling band of rowdy cowhands, looking for relief from the winds, came upon them. They were taken as prisoners, and bound with a precision that said this was not the first time the cowhands had behaved in such a manner.

Their thick-bellied leader, whose one distinguishing feature was a pirate's patch covering his left eye, said in a voice thick with malice, "Okay, boys, y'all know the rules of the game. Who wins first goes first after me, then the rest of you rowdies in order of winning can choose between the lady and her gent." He made a show of indecision before pointing at Jeanne. "She's my choice, boys, like you didn't figger that out for yourselfs already."

Swaney reacted at once. "You keep your filthy hands off her, range trash, or live to regret it."

"You hear that, boys? Like he has any say in the matter." The leader fired his boot, catching Swaney in the stomach and causing him to cry out in pain. "You watch us now, loudmouth," he said. "Ain't only my filthy hands that'll be adjusting how the lady looks at life anymore."

Jeanne knew better than to resist. This wasn't the first time she'd been assaulted, only this time the gents weren't paying her for the privilege. Neither were the cowhands next in line, trading expressions in a game that made no sense to her.

One might say *Lazy Left Up R* and be answered *Diamond and a Half.*

Or the response to *Hay Hook* might be *Bradded Y.*

They carried on endlessly, Jeanne the winner's choice most of the time.

After a while, the leader called: *Tumbling Ladder.* It signaled his men no longer had to choose between Jeanne and Swaney. They were free to have a whack at both.

Swaney's body became a punching bag even after he slipped into unconsciousness, the cowhands endeavoring to outdo one another on their way to enjoying Jeanne, most for a third or fourth turn.

Jeanne closed her eyes and endured, stoic until the windstorm quit and the cowhands prepared to travel on.

"Leave what's left of him for the coyotes, but she's coming with us," the leader said.

"No, never," Jeanne said.

"Small tall Wall," he called, smacked her across the face, and dragged her from the cave, winning loud huzzahs from his men.

Swaney was struggling to regain his senses. He heard: "Lowell! Lowell! Dear God!

70

Lowell!" He had no idea who was screaming or what the words meant.

A scouting party of outcast redskins called
"Wandering Jutes" stumbled across a half-
dead Swaney in the cave while hunting for
fresh meat.

"What's your story, white man?" the half-
breed among them said.

Swaney, struggling to keep his swollen
eyes open, tried telling the half-breed he
had no idea who he was, where he was, or
how he got there.

He couldn't get the words out.

The sounds he made bore no resemblance
to understandable English.

The half-breed reported this to his chief,
Deer in the Water, a heavily wrinkled old
man in his late nineties, who smiled a tooth-
less smile. "Prepare a drag cot," the chief
said. "We take the white man with us."

"Is that wise, most honorable and vener-
ated chief? We are entering the land of
Skunkers. They are treacherous enemies.
Anything slowing us down represents a
danger to life and limb."

"Are you turning coward, my son?"

"You know better."

"Do you find the prospect of starving to
death superior to defending our honor on

the plains of battle?"

"I've always proven myself to your satisfaction, have I not?"

"You have, so consider — our food stores are dwindling. Should it become necessary, this white man you found represents more than enough meat to feed our people for three or four days after we have passed out of Skunkers territory and the danger it represents."

"Of course. How foolish of me to question your wisdom, but tell me, didn't you put a rule in place some time ago that forbids us to any longer taste of human flesh?"

"Rules are made to be broken, my son."

They were almost to safe ground when Skunkers emerged from hiding places behind bushes and boulders and the hills above them, dozens on foot and horseback, waving weapons and shouting their intention to destroy the trespassers.

The Wandering Jutes, never ones to fear battle, prepared to face the Skunkers once Swaney's drag cot was hidden from discovery under a mound of taft branches and fetis leaves, the old chief determined to protect this important food source at all costs.

They suffered casualties, but somehow managed to win the battle over odds that at first seemed overwhelming.

The chief was unable to control his anger when he learned the drag cot was nowhere to be found and not one of his people able to explain how it had gone missing. He had them scour the area for hours, to no avail. "I sense our gods have other plans for the white man," the chief said. "So be it. We move on."

The dime weeklies never agreed on the exact details, but they were confident about crediting Swaney's survival to his discovery by an Injun girl who also was trespassing. She spotted the drag cot in the heat of battle and, unnoticed, moved it to her safe cabin in the hills, where she already was tending to the needs of another white man.

Unwittingly, she had reunited Swaney and McDukes.

Her name was Flowing Beaver, and she came to love them both.

Or only Swaney.

Or only McDukes.

CHAPTER 7

Even after Swaney was healed and well enough to speak, his memory continued to deprive him of his name or other clues to his identity.

McDukes was no better off.

In conversation they took to calling the other *Mister.*

It made no difference to Flowing Beaver.

In the beginning, she neither understood nor spoke any language other than her own tongue, which defied understanding by Swaney or McDukes.

She came to think of McDukes as "Hidden Darkness."

Swaney became "Secret Sun."

They referred to her as their "copper-toned saint" sometimes, the "redskin" or, more often, the "Injun girl."

She was not pretty, only acceptable in looks, but she radiated an inner beauty that spoke to a purity of soul surprising to

74

discover in someone so young, in her mid-twenties at most, and hardened by the burdens of prairie life. Her winning smile turned its brightest after Secret Sun and Hidden Darkness entered into constant conversation, mainly to share the common goal of pleasing her. They competed for her attention and affection and, in time, came to love her.

They never spoke of marrying her one day, but that's what each believed the future held.

It showed in how they acted toward Flowing Beaver.

Together or alone, they were good to her, respectful, always returning kindness with kindness. For her part, there was nothing to suggest she was even aware of the competition. She taught them the sign language of her people. In return, Hidden Darkness and Secret Sun began teaching her English, using a well-worn Bible charred around the edges that they discovered languishing under a pile of blankets.

Hidden Darkness said, "Where did it come from?"

"Wandering Jute," she said.

"They gave you the Bible?"

"Only him. One Jute who no give," and with that attempt at English, Flowing Beaver resorted to sign language to tell the story.

Last year, she had stumbled across the Jute, severely wounded while fighting off a pack of wolves, and carried him to the safety of her cabin, much as she would come to rescue Hidden Darkness and Secret Sun.

The Jute died in her arms.

The Bible was in his pouch.

She threw it into the fireplace,

It wouldn't burn, so she tossed it aside.

It was an exceptionally cruel winter. The snow made travel impossible. Her food supply ran out. If she didn't do something to remedy the situation, she'd be dead before too many more moons passed. She thought about feeding on pages from the Bible before rejecting the notion in favor of another one.

The Jute.

She would feast on the Jute.

His people were widely known as eaters of human flesh, so how bad could it be?

The idea excited her.

She would risk it.

She prepared the Jute for roasting much as she would ready a rabbit, a squirrel, or a buck, growing more and more anxious to discover if his flavor would be equal to any one of those meat dishes.

He tasted more like chicken.

She liked chicken, she revealed to Secret Sun and Hidden Darkness; then she silenced her hands and used one to sweep away the saliva puddling at the corners of her mouth.

Secret Sun reacted to Flowing Beaver's story with wide-eyed amazement.

Hidden Darkness struggled to keep from vomiting.

But neither thought any less of her.

How Flowing Beaver felt toward them remained her secret.

Time passed.

The weather cleared and the men were healthy enough to leave Flowing Beaver's cabin and resume their journeys. They still had no idea where they were meant to be before losing their memory, but sure they had had enough of one another to go their separate ways.

First one and then the other invited Flowing Beaver to join him.

"Not one," she said, and held up two fingers. "Both."

They couldn't convince her otherwise and gave in.

She set off the next morning and returned hours later with two mustangs and a colt she had discovered wandering aimlessly in a wooded section of the flatlands, no evidence of their riders or how they got there.

The trio headed off west, the direction chosen by Secret Sun after he won the toss of a coin. About a half mile out, they heard what sounded like an explosion and saw fire and smoke climbing the sky from the area of Flowing Beaver's cabin.

"Must go back and see," she said as she turned around and sped off, Hidden Darkness and Secret Sun close on her tail.

The cabin was engulfed in flames, beyond saving.

Flowing Beaver wept.

Later, sifting through the ruins for salvage, all they found worth saving was a scorched Bible.

"It's a sign a-something," Hidden Darkness said.

Secret Sun agreed. "Like telling us we were lucky cusses to be gone from here before the fire, or our goose would of been cooked a lot worse than that Jute she told us about."

"And come away tasting like chicken."

"More like lamb or something else, our being white meat, not redskins."

Flowing Beaver made a face. She didn't understand humor was often the white man's way of dealing with sadness and

78

tragedy. She fled their company. Hidden Darkness and Secret Sun vaulted onto their mustangs and caught up with her.

They got as far as a fork in the road and had stopped to make a choice, when trouble stepped out from the shadows of the possum trees and ordered them at gunpoint to dismount and drop their weapons.

It was Denny Slime under the Sugar Loaf sombrero he wore at a rakish angle, the one and same gunslinger for hire who Cactus Billy Clemens, at McDukes's urging, had paid, along with Juan Forminfante, to find and dispose of Lowell Swaney.

Now here they were, McDukes and Swaney, sharing the same trail with some pigtailed Injun girlie, looking like the best of friends. Slime was confused, and said so. "I am confused," he said. "What's going on here, McDukes? Some change of heart you never told me about?"

Secret Sun and Hidden Darkness had no sense what he was talking about or to whom he was speaking.

Denny Slime was cross-eyed. He seemed to be looking at one of them, but addressing the other.

He said, "I don't know your game, McDukes, but you need to 'fess up, play straight with this Yankee boy and his beaner partner, Juan, who right now's after Swaney down another trail."

"He means you," Hidden Darkness said.

"Seems to me he has his sight set on you," Secret Sun said.

Denny Slime said, "Let's hear it, McDukes. My patience is beginning to run thinner than my dear mother's sewing thread."

Flowing Beaver had been waiting for an opportunity to catch this bad man off-guard. Here it was, while his eyes were playing tricks between Secret Sun and Hidden Darkness. She dismounted, uncoiled with the speed of a rattler, and sprang at Slime.

Straddled him.

Smashed her thumbs deep into his eyes and ripped at his throat with her teeth.

Slime pushed her off him, stumbled backward onto the dirt, and, gushing blood, was dead within minutes.

Flowing Beaver celebrated by performing a short tribal victory dance that left her bent over, hands gripping her knees while she caught her breath.

"We can leave now again," she said, "but first one other thing. What those names he call you by?"

Secret Sun said, "He called me Swaney."

"No," Hidden Darkness said. "McDukes

80

he said to you and Swaney to me."

Unable to agree, their memories still inaccessible, they handed Flowing Beaver a coin.

Hidden Darkness won the toss.

"No question about it now," he said. "I am Swaney, making you McDukes, McDukes."

Secret Sun could not mask his anger, declaring, "I hate the name, but I accept the result. McDukes it is, until the day arrives we get confirmation or maybe hear other names to be the truth."

"What's in a name anyway?" Swaney said.

Or, maybe, it was McDukes.

With that reasonably settled, they had Flowing Beaver toss the coin again, this time to determine which trail to follow.

It led them to Atonement.

CHAPTER 8

Atonement thrived in its day, before the bulk of the resident population moved bag and baggage down the road to Salvation.

What caused the mass exodus?

Gold, of course.

The Atonement deposits had run down to a trickle, whereas the deposits in aptly named Salvation had begun turning struggling slate miners into millionaires.

The dying township suited perfectly the current needs of Swaney and McDukes.

They discovered an abandoned cabin short of a mile from the center of Atonement and moved in with Flowing Beaver, who set about putting their new home in order while they took off to explore the town.

They had paused for drinks and sweet rolls at the Keepers Coffee House when they were approached by a middle-aged gent, tall and broad-shouldered, wearing a

82

slightly tattered Union blue officer's uniform. He carried himself with military bearing and spoke in a brusque manner that suggested familiarity with command.

He was the coffeehouse owner, Colonel Francis Milstead Keepers.

Legend had it he was unhorsed during the Battle of Mahoney's Bend, and he hid from the enemy by blanketing himself under a fallen comrade. He then crawled out of sight along the banks of a shallow creek, finally downstream to safety by hanging onto a log of passing deadwood. Feats of folly and heroism that subsequently made their way into print were all thought up by writers surviving on pennies a word from Beadle and the other pulps.

"Swaney," Keepers called out, as he dropped to his knees and clasped his hands as if in prayer. "I beg of you — please don't kill me."

"What's makes you think I even want to?" said the cowboy standing next to Swaney,

"Not you," Keepers said. "Him."

"Same question applies from me, old-timer, but first — my name's McDukes. Who are you?"

Keepers couldn't understand their game, playacting like — like — like they didn't know who they were.

"Colonel Francis Milstead Keepers. You don't know me?"

"Why should we?"

Keepers put his reply to both of them, turning it into a test. "Maybe you should get the reason from Ellie."

"L.E.? Don't recognize those initials. How about you, McDukes?"

"Rings no bells for me neither, Swaney. You got a last name goes with them, Colonel?"

Keepers was convinced. He picked himself up and straightened his jacket. "Afraid I don't. Besides, I was only joking around. Tell me, you boys here for the duration or is this a quick stop on your way to Salvation?"

"We're settled in for now, a cabin down the road apiece, and got us a stash of gold and cash money to last for a long while, so there's no hurry to decide."

"Then welcome to Atonement from the town's mayor himself, boys. You do decide to stick around, I'm prepared to offer you attractive jobs available for a reasonable cost, exclusive of mine, of course, and far better than you will ever find in Salvation."

That sparked their interest.

Swaney said, "I noticed a gaming parlor coming into town. Wouldn't mind taking it on."

"Being town sheriff appeals to me," McDukes said.

Keepers threw out prices with built-in room for negotiation, but presented like he was doing Swaney and McDukes a favor.

They bit without argument or a moment's thought, leading the colonel to think he could have successfully quoted twice as much; also to wonder if they were more familiar with his past than they had let on.

No, probably not, he concluded, or he'd be dead right now, same as McDukes.

Lonely Todd Logan appeared after Swaney and McDukes drifted away. He was barely five-five in height with hooded bloodshot eyes that reflected venom and a mouth stuffed with chewing tobacco that interfered with the ability to understand him half the time.

Logan had heard the entire conversation unobserved and was seething.

"Dammit, Colonel, you give away my job as town sheriff," he said.

"This McDukes or Swaney, whichever he is, he bought it fair and square for a princely sum, Todd. You got enough money to buy it back?"

"You know better'n that."

"Then go be his deputy."

"What if instead I kill him? I have it back then?"

"Then you would have your own funeral. You don't know about Swaney and McDukes, talk seriously about taking them on, you deserve to be a dead man."

"And you?"

"They had a clear mind for who they were, I'd already be getting fitted for a coffin. I get a feeling they've turned wise to me. I will get rid of them without damage to our own skins."

Logan aimed a wad of chaw at the nearest spittoon and missed. "The copper lady, she also gets sent to her happy hunting grounds?"

"An Injun? What's that about?"

"I was passing by the old Lowy cabin when them boys come on out, leaving her waving goodbye from the porch, them waving back," Logan said. "How it is I come to trail after them, curious to know why they took on the cabin and what it might mean for the safety and well-being of our town and its people." He tried another shot at the spittoon and missed again. "Don't look now, Colonel, but there's the squaw herself."

Flowing Beaver was standing at the coffee shop entrance.

Keepers and Logan had no way knowing for how long or how much of their conversation she'd overheard. Not much, actually, given her limited command of English.

She smiled.

They smiled back.

She nodded.

They nodded back.

She smiled again.

They smiled again.

She said, "Come look for Swaney."

"Not here anymore," the colonel said, making every word a sentence.

"McDukes?" she said.

"Not him neither. They friends of yours?"

"Friends of yours," she said, repeating his words. "Me go look more."

She turned and left.

Keepers took a deep breath and let it out slowly. "What do you make out she heard, Logan?"

Logan ripped off a fresh chunk of Jolly Jack's and stuffed his mouth. "Everything, I figure. You hear her call them friends of ours?"

"If their squaw bitch knows that much, they must be playing some kind of game on me. They are candidates for Boot Hill and the sooner the better."

"How?"

87

"Quit the Injun talk. Get over to Salvation, find Leaukomia, and tell him I got a nice piece of work for him that pays out twice his usual and a bonus for the squaw."

"If anyone can do in Swaney and McDukes, it's Pronto."

'You still here?'

"On my way," Logan said. He attempted the spittoon one more time; missed.

CHAPTER 9

Pronto took the job, figuring it would be fast work and solve the money problems he was having because of a bad run of luck at the card tables.

The next day, heading for the cabin described by Lonely Todd Logan, he resembled a lumbering bear in a bearskin overcoat and a hairy cap of Injun scalps meant to keep him warm against the frigid late afternoon air.

Swaney and McDukes didn't seem to be around. Their horses were gone, but not their squaw. Pronto spotted her through the cabin window cooking some sort of sweet-smelling stew. He figured to kill her now, then help himself to some of that stew while waiting for the cowpokes to return.

He barged into the cabin with his Bowie knife drawn.

Flowing Beaver had spotted Pronto peeking at her and was waiting for him with her shotgun drawn.

He skidded to a stop and turned to flee as she fired.

Her aim was true.

He stumbled, but his heavy overcoat saved him from serious damage.

He swung around cursing Flowing Beaver, more determined than ever to finish her off.

Only now she had a revolver aimed at him.

No way was he going to outrun a bullet.

He dropped his Bowie and unhitched his gun belt.

She had Pronto stretched out on his back on the cabin's dirt floor and was keeping steady watch over him, one hand gripping the revolver, the Bowie in her other hand, when Swaney and McDukes returned.

McDukes took over guarding him, freeing Flowing Beaver to describe what happened in sign language.

"That an accurate accounting, Leaukomia?"

"How should I know? Your squaw wasn't talkin' no language I understand, an' how do you come off knowin' my name anyhow?"

"I seen it and your ugly mug on enough wanted posters to make a lasting impression is how I know."

"And I know about Swaney and McDukes the same way, so that puts us even. You got no objection to my sitting up, I'd be most obliged."

"You move, you dead. Otherwise no objection."

Pronto held his pose.

"Tell me in the tongue we both understand better," McDukes said. "What's this about?"

"What do I get in return?"

"Your life," Swaney said, "and we keep our sweet little Injun girl, who happens to be one fine cook, from turning you into chops and spare ribs. Sound like a fair deal, Leaukomia?"

"You wouldn't."

"That a gamble you want to take? You got 'til three to make up your mind. One. Two —"

Leaukomia told them everything.

McDukes's face reddened and his voice turned into a growl. "I'm out to get that bastard colonel right this minute," he said. "You stay here and look after Flowing Beaver and this here murderous galoot, Swaney."

"I ain't about to do so, McDukes. You go, I go. That's the way it's going to play out."

Leaukomia chipped in his two pennies'

91

worth. "Would be easier on me you boys let me up, maybe tie me good and tight to that chair over there so's I ain't going away anytime soon."

"Where you go we'll figure out when we get back," McDukes said, "but roping you up good and tight is a fair request."

Flowing Beaver understood what they were talking about. "Go both and I be fine," she said in English and sign language. "He trying anything, I kill."

The colonel hadn't been around the Keepers Coffee House or anywhere else in town for hours, were McDukes and Swaney to buy the word of Lonely Todd Logan, who was well into his cups on more than coffee.

"Where'd he run off to?" McDukes said.

"No idea, Sheriff."

"When's he coming back?"

"Bein' the boss of this here town, the colonel comes and goes as he pleases, no questions allowed and no answers given." Logan took aim at the spittoon, fired, and missed. "Anything I can do you for, seeing I stepped down as sheriff to make room for you, becoming your deputy in the bargain."

"You get back to me the minute Keepers shows his stripe, can you do that, Logan?"

"I can and I will, Sheriff. Take my word for it."

"Actions speak louder'n words, Deputy."

"Then you'll hear me screaming whenever it counts," Logan said. "I got yer back covered fer sure." He made a fresh try for the spittoon. Missed.

They hadn't been gone long from the cabin, but it was long enough to discover Pronto Leaukomia had somehow managed to escape, taking Flowing Beaver with him.

"I'm plugging that sumbitch for certain next time, no heaven to help him he's so much as laid a gesture on that little prairie flower of ours," Swaney said. "You hole up here while I go on the hunt, in case Pronto comes back looking for us."

"Him and her, they would still be here you stuck around like I wanted, but you did not," McDukes said. "I'm going off without you this time, so save any arguments for somebody else. I plan to corral Pronto and see him hung after they build a scaffold, march the lowlife bastard out to meet his maker, and spring the trap."

Swaney was still arguing otherwise about going when McDukes turned to leave, calling to his backside: "You're one stubborn mule, McDukes, worst I ever come across my whole life. Get yourself gunned down, it'll serve you right."

McDukes stopped off at the coffeehouse and waved Lonely Todd Logan over.

"Sheriff, I don't need no checking up," Logan said. "I'm off the sauce an' on the case one hunnert percent. No sign of the colonel or you'da heard from me by now."

"Not that, Logan. I'm going on the hunt for Leaukomia, who took off with our Injun girl. Need someone along who knows the territory better than me and can steer me straight. Thought you might be that man."

"I'm your man," Logan said, "an' pleased for the chance to show myself worthy of the tin star I'm wearin' as your deputy." He proposed they head for Salvation, where Leaukomia spent considerable time when he wasn't off plundering elsewhere. "The Difficult Bends trail is rough, but a shortcut that gets us there in a hurry."

"As good as any guess I got," McDukes said.

They headed off, but two hours out the trail proved a wrong choice when shots rang out and bullets came dangerously close, forcing them to dash for cover in the tall and unruly brush, ready to trade fire with their unseen adversaries.

94

The shooting stopped as fast as it began.

A nasty, threatening voice called from across the road: "We got you covered every which way, travelers, including men up there on the bluff behind you. Throw us your weapons and your treasures, send your horses over to us, and we'll let you walk away unharmed."

Loud enough to cause an echo, McDukes said, "You lie between your words. We do what you say, we're dead men for certain, so no thank you. We'll fight to the death, taking as many of you with us as possible."

"Who taught you those foolish words, General Custer? Give in and give up. Surrender and live. I'll give you a few minutes to think it through, but that's all."

McDukes turned to Lonely Todd Logan. "I won't hold you to my decision, Logan. You want to chance doing what's asked and walk away unscathed, now's the time, an' I won't think less of you."

"Maybe you will after you hear my confession, Sheriff. I knew what the colonel had in mind for you and Swaney, was me give Leaukomia directions to the cabin, or your Injun girl would still be around and none of this happening."

McDukes closed his eyes to his deputy and briefly seemed at war with himself.

95

"Save any confessing for a priest, Logan. I admire you for coming out with the truth. Far as I'm considered, it moves you to the right side of the law."

Logan, dewy-eyed, dug his teeth into a fresh chew, and made the sign of the cross. "Then I'm with you all the way, Sheriff. Better to think of myself as a dead hero than a live coward."

The nasty voice called out: "Need your answer right now, cowboy. You are clear out of time."

Someone new entered the standoff. "Hold on, Heck. I thought the voice I been hearing was too familiar to come from a stranger."

"You saying you know him, Buchanan?"

"Know him? Was me what helped bust him out of Desert Prison, which puts him on our side of law'n order. You know your dime weeklies, you'd see his picture for who he is, Lowell Swaney hisself." He stepped empty-handed into the clearing. "It's me, Ned Buchanan. C'mon out. Nothin' to fear no more."

McDukes said, "It's him all right, Logan. I know Buchanan's ugly puss, recognize that gutter voice. He's a man to be trusted."

"Then how come he got your name

wrong, Sheriff. Could be a trick of some sort."

"Probably because we haven't conversed in a long time's the reason he made the mistake. Anyway, I'm ripe to chance it, an' you come along or not as you please." He called: "Stepping out with my arms raised to the sky, Buchanan."

"Shit," Logan said, and followed behind him.

They converged in the middle of the trail. Logan breathed easier as McDukes and Ned Buchanan hugged, backslapped, and laughed over the curious way their reunion had come about.

Cowpokes emerged from every point of the ambush. One in particular, packing two revolvers and a military-issue rifle, moved in on Buchanan and McDukes. Buchanan introduced him as Heck Jarman. He stood tall and broad-shouldered and carried command in his widespread eyes, where the rest of his jowly face was distinguished only by his bulbous, blue-veined nose.

Jarman said, "Ned vouches for you, otherwise we would be trading bullets now. Frankly, you don't look like you do in the weeklies, where you look to me more like your partner on the run from prison, Swaney by name."

"They got it wrong. I'm McDukes for certain. Tell him, Ned."

Buchanan took a step back and confirmed for himself he was looking at Swaney. He had called him by his correct name. He had no idea why he was passing himself off as McDukes, but Swaney was nobody's fool. There had to be good reason for the deception.

Buchanan said, "My mistake, Heck. McDukes knows who his mother is better'n the magazines or me."

"One other thing then. If like you say he's on our side of law'n order, explain the tin stars him and his friend are wearing."

Before McDukes could frame an answer, Logan spoke up: "We took them off'n a pair of lawmen who won't be chasing after us no more," he said.

"Coming at you for what reason?"

"A disagreement at the card table, where this gamblin' man drew to an inside straight once too often, got called on his cheatin' ways by me, and thought to take on McDukes, not realizin' he'd be goin' against the best shot in the territory."

Buchanan agreed. "Maybe a tie with Lowell Swaney, but none faster I ever seen," he said.

"Neither ever come up against me, and so

what?" Jarman said. "Welcome to our ranks, boys."

About the same time, Colonel Keepers trooped back to Atonement leading a modest squad of former military men who once served under his command. The dime weeklies would later speculate he had assembled them to do his bidding after visiting the cabin to determine if Pronto Leaukomia had succeeded in disposing of Swaney and McDukes and their Injun squaw.

The cabin was empty, except for signs of a modest scuffle, no evidence Leaukomia was due his payoff. As was the case many times over in past years, the colonel decided to take on the task for himself, thus guaranteeing success and in the bargain saving himself the hefty sum he'd promised Leaukomia.

To his surprise, he found Swaney hefting a beer at his gaming parlor. Getting rid of the troublesome pair, starting with Swaney, was going to be easier than he thought. He put his men on alert, and suppressed a sly smile, asking, "Where's that partner of yours?"

"McDukes? He's on the trail of a dirty, miserable rat who done us wrong, Keepers by name, Colonel Francis Milstead Keepers."

"You saying me, Swaney?"

"Only if you recognize the description."

"I invite you to step outside and remark like that."

"Where you got your boys ready to gun me down and pass it off for your own bravery? I don't think so. One against one's my idea of a fair shuffle."

"Then so be it." Keepers pressed a palm to his heart. "You have my word."

"How do I know the words I just heard from you are not yours, only some you borrowed just for this occasion?"

"A coward's retreat. You change your mind, I'll be waiting," the colonel said, clearly a taunt. Outside, he called for someone to stand in his stead. "Take that mutt down and it's a triple bonus."

"I'm for that," Corporal South Templeton said. He dismounted and marched to a midway spot in the dung-infected street trail fronting the gaming parlor.

"A foolish decision," someone in the pack called out. "If that's the Swaney I know, it's like buying your own death certificate."

"Who claims that? Speak up!" the colonel said.

"Right here, Colonel. Ruben Garner by

name. Called 'Rube' by those I know." He was sitting tall on a tired bronc, soft-spoken, square-jawed, and steely-eyed, looking every inch like he belonged punching cattle on the open range, the way he would come to be pictured in the pages of the Frank Leslie dime bibles.

"Do I know you?"

"Not likely, Colonel. New to your pack. Fell in for the coin, not for any happy memory of past campaigns. Didn't know where this would lead or I wouldn't be here now."

"You talk like you're some friend of Swaney, or maybe his absent partner, McDukes, or even their squaw. Is that what you're all about Ruben Garner?"

Garner rolled a cigarette and drew a flame from the stick match he fired up with a thumb snap, filled his lungs, and blew out a string of smoke rings. "I'm about fairness, Colonel, and, from what I observe, there's nothing fair happening here on your part."

"I'm the only one whose opinion matters, Garner, so you are dismissed," the colonel said. "You ready, Corporal Templeton?"

"As I'll ever be, sir." He gave his holster a few love pats and practiced his quick draw twice. He was fast, maybe even a fair match for Swaney.

Keepers called: "Swaney, you wanted one against one and I'm obliging you. Come out and face your future."

Time momentarily seemed to stand still after his declaration, but that changed after Swaney stepped into the doorway and saw Templeton waiting for him. "Glory be to Hell," he said. "I got nothin' against you, cowboy. Do yourself a favor an' don't play substitute for that damn colonel."

"No hard feelings on my end, but I can use the payday home, where I got the wife and children going through hardship," Templeton said.

"Won't get any easier for them if you're dead an' buried, cowboy."

"Thanks, but I got other plans."

"Suit yourself," Swaney said. He met Templeton in the street. They turned back-to-back and began walking in opposite directions to a count of ten in traditional showdown fashion, the steps called out by the colonel. On ten, both men swung around, weapons in hand, and seemed to fire at the same time.

Templeton's bullet raced past Swaney and bit the dirt.

Swaney's aim was more accurate.

Templeton appeared to lift off the ground and hover in the air before he slammed down face forward dead on the muddy trail.

Swaney holstered his Colt. "Any more candidates?" he said.

In response, the street came alive with gunfire, Swaney the target.

When it ceased, the street was littered with bodies.

The colonel wasn't one of them.

Neither was Swaney.

He had shot his way back into the gaming parlor, already occupied by Ruben Garner and someone he took for Lonely Todd Logan. "Logan, what are you doing here when you're meant to be off with McDukes tracking after Pronto Leaukomia?"

"You got me confused with my twin, Lonely Todd, cowboy. I'm called Little Tad Logan by them what know me good enough to tell the difference." He blew a wad of chewing tobacco at a spittoon and scored.

"One of Keepers's boys, are you?"

"Yes an' no. More no than yes. Signed on not so long ago, mainly for the company on the trail ride here for a visit with Todd, not for what's currently happening."

"I can vouch for that," Ruben Garner said. "Last we talked, Little Tad, you were bragging on how well you know the territory, even better than Lonely Todd."

"Like a cloud knows its limits, Rube, but

I'm no expert on expelling us from the kind of pickle we're in right now."

Swaney said, "We shoot our way out, of course, or my name ain't Lowell Swaney."

"It may be your name, but it ain't who you are," Garner said.

"Say again?"

"No disrespect and don't know the game you're into, but I'm ready to put my hand on the Bible and testify you're McDukes."

Swaney seemed startled by Garner's pronouncement. He had a memory of hearing that once before, but bullets started crashing through the walls and windows before he could respond.

Little Tad shouted, "What say we pick them off before they kill us?" He posted himself at a window and fired back.

Garner used another window, as did Swaney, who called to him over the gunfire: "Then who is McDukes if you're saying I'm him?"

"He's the true Lowell Swaney," Garner said. "You'll hear everything it is I know if we somehow manage to survive this shoot-out." He answered a shot that whizzed dangerously close to his ear.

"Got me another one!" Little Tad Logan said.

"Put me down for two more by any

name," Swaney said, and fired again. "Make that three more."

Obscured by the gunfire were the fearful sounds of the terrified woman protecting herself behind an overturned Faro table.

CHAPTER 10

The real Swaney was still calling himself McDukes the first night he and Lonely Todd Logan settled into camp with Heck Jarman and his men, unaware Jarman was troubled by the question of identity and close to leaving them for the wolves to feast on come morning.

Ned Buchanan managed to find a few minutes to engage Swaney in private conversation and warn him. "I know Heck to be a man of honor, whose word is pure gold," he said, "but he's bothered by you hiding your true identity. You need to drop this name game you're playing and own up to being Lowell Swaney."

"Logan and I thank you for your concern, but Sean McDukes is who I am, and you know that for a fact if you know me from Desert Prison or before. Making myself out to be Swaney or someone else would be the lie, and I'm not one for living with lies."

Buchanan threw up his hands and left him, grumbling, beginning to wonder if, maybe, it was his own memory playing tricks on him.

He next put the question to Logan. "He's always been McDukes to me," Logan said. "We left Swaney in Atonement and we've been making tracks ever since on the hunt after Pronto Leaukomia and an Injun girl both got reasons to favor."

Bedded down for the night, Buchanan's thoughts drifted to the Lowell Swaney who rode with McDukes.

Swaney was all macho then, always dressed in a white suit that came to identify him as much as his blazing guns. Earlier, in the cavalry and as a private scout for hire, he had chosen the baggy trousers and jacket over the gaudy blue britches and shiny buttons of standard army issue, his gun belt cinched tight to hold a pair of custom-crafted leather holsters.

Damn, he was fast on the draw, more or less the equal of McDukes, and they would joke about it, each claiming superiority, although neither saw any reason to ever put it to the test. This was before the issue of McDukes's dead wife came between them.

Buchanan was often asked who might emerge the winner of a showdown, but he refused to speculate, always responding: "One of them would win, but both of them would lose."

This wasn't the Swaney of memory he was seeing, but it was Swaney for sure, traveling as McDukes and hiding the truth from everyone, even from himself.

So be it. Buchanan would play the game, too, rather than be the cause of Swaney's death at the hands of Heck Jarman.

He sought out Jarman in the morning. "Heck, talking to both, I'm positive the mistake was mine, my memory as old as the rest of me. It's McDukes for certain, and him and Logan also got their loyalty turned to your command, so you can relax your concerns."

"You say so, Ned, I'm satisfied," Jarman said. "It turns out otherwise for any reason, be forewarned you'll be put down alongside them for steering me in the wrong direction."

Were one to believe the dime weeklies, Jarman's trust in Buchanan, stronger than with others, came to fill some gap sometime after the real Lowell Swaney stole Jeanne d'Evreaux and fled New Testament with her, barely ahead of a posse nipping at his tail and the hired killers, Denny Slime and

Juan Forminfante.

It began in a town called Scuffers Meadow, a stretch of land the size of a small state that had been claimed as their kingdom by a militant band of settlers controlled by a messianic fire-and-brimstone leader of deceptively modest appearance, known to these "Scuffers" as "Old Man Dekker."

Dekker was dedicated to the eradication of cattlemen and sheep farmers, anyone who dared claim title to so much as an acre. Doing so was sufficient cause for warfare. The Scuffers lost men and more than a few women who took up arms, but they never lost the battle.

Buntline himself printed an interview with Old Man Dekker, in which Dekker said: "If they come after us hard and fast, we will survive to sport their backsides yonder. We have no beef, we pull no wool. We grow like Scuffers plain and on the mark, trucking neither malice nor interference by our intent, but pity them what seek to turn our slumber into wake. We'll do the trick ourselves and give them rest they'll never know or covet, however eased their muscles and our minds."

Dekker first uttered the words ministering at a Sunday potluck service. They proved so inspiring, he was urged to repeat them at least once a month, a thirty-day period of worship he created from half of April and half of May.

Buchanan rode into Scuffers Meadow innocent of this history or the absolute control Dekker wielded and searched out the town's one saloon. He had been on the trail for days. His thirst needed quenching.

He got drunk, stumbled out of the saloon, and wandered to an area behind the stables, where he was discovered by one of Old Man Dekker's lieutenants and led off to a jail cell to sober up before facing the wrath of Dekker for violating one of Scuffers Meadows's top twenty commandments: *Thou shalt not drink harsh spirits to oblivion.*

Buchanan was indifferent to his status, still deeply troubled at having overheard the real McDukes inspire the deal that put Forminfante and Slime on a death hunt for Swaney. He didn't know yet that Slime was dead and, worse, the doing of an Injun squaw who had taken a fancy to both Swaney and McDukes.

Of immediate concern was discovering Forminfante a prisoner in another cell, when the hired killer called over to him: "I know you, you old fart, so I don't have to guess you know me, Ned Buchanan."

Buchanan held no truck for Forminfante.

He turned over on his cot, showing him his backside, and feigned sleep until a prisoner in the next cell said, "He was talking to you, old-timer, so you might extend him some courtesy."

"My ass is all the courtesy he deserves," Buchanan said. He rolled over and recognized the speaker from his wanted picture on post office and law office walls. "You ain't as pretty as your wanteds, Heck Jarman."

"I know, I know, and I resent it. They get it right next time or I find and kill the man what put the inky line to paper."

"Your first victim should of been Mother Nature for giving you that face to begin with," Buchanan said.

Jarman's laughter rocked the jailhouse. "I've killed men for saying less about me, but I like you, Buchanan. Not that many are brave like you been facing me."

"Honest and foolhardy is more like it," Buchanan said, earning an even louder guffaw.

"Yes siree, bob. You stay honest that way and me'n you gonna be great friends once we clear outta this town and the crazy keep of Old Man Dekker."

"You saying you have escape on your mind?"

111

"It's either that or the rope Dekker has planned for my neck as punishment for breaking one of his commandments."

"I'm guessing you killed somebody."

"No. Like I said, for breaking one of his commandments, 'Thou shalt not.' "

"Shalt not what?"

"He never did say. Just that I broke it, bringing down shame on Scuffers Meadows, and that made it a hanging offense."

"What kind of escape?"

"My boys will come rescue me if I ain't back by midday tomorrow."

"Suppose your hanging comes in the morning. What then?"

The question startled Jarman. "I hadn't looked that far ahead."

"Then hear me out," Buchanan said. He recited his skills at planning and carrying out escapes, using McDukes and Swaney as his most recent example, and described what he had in mind for them.

"Ain't that too obvious, something that happens all the time?"

"Exactly. It's so obvious they always figure they're too smart for it to happen to them."

"Buchanan, you spring us, you are safe under my wing for however long you choose. When do we start?"

"No time like the present, Heck."

112

Jarman dropped to the cell floor and began moaning and groaning.

At once Buchanan yelled for the deputy on duty to do something about the ailment that struck down Jarman without warning.

The deputy entered Jarman's cell to check on the prisoner's condition.

A few minutes later, the deputy was unconscious and hogtied on the cell floor and Jarman and Buchanan were heading out from the jailhouse.

"Hey, *amigos,* what about me?" Juan Forminfante shouted. They ignored him. "I won't forget this, especially not you, Buchanan. You already a dead man in my book."

A week after Swaney, believing he was McDukes, was captured by Jarman and had his identity vouched for by Buchanan, Jarman decided to put his loyalty to the test. "I don't doubt your word on him, Ned, but I need to find out firsthand for myself where McDukes stands. Any objections your part?"

"You're the boss, Heck. What do you have in mind for him?"

"Remember how you and me first met up in Scuffers Meadow an' that business with Old Man Dekker that wudda got me hung

113

'cept fer you?"

"How could I not, seeing as how you mention it almost every day?"

"Paying Dekker back for that slight is overdue, so I'm dispatching McDukes to take care of that business with a well-placed bullet or two that sends the crazy old man to meet his maker."

"McDukes was never the one to kill without a cause of his own, Heck."

"Well, he is now, to prove his damn loyalty to me, or else. He don't get the job done, he's finished by my reckoning."

"What if McDukes doesn't come back?"

"I told him it's goodbye then for his little pal Logan, and maybe you, for steering me wrong about them two in the first place."

McDukes didn't return.

After more than enough days had passed, Jarman prepared to march Lonely Todd Logan in front of a firing squad.

Buchanan gambled. He said, "Also me, Heck. You named me in your warning, so I'm ready to pay the piper alongside Logan."

Jarman toned down his anger and gave Buchanan's words hard thought. "Changed my mind concerns you, Ned. Your friendship allows you this one misjudgment."

"Thank you, but no, Heck. I have too

114

much respect for you and your leadership to not give you the loyalty you deserve as my final act on God's good green earth, besides —"

"Besides what? Let's hear it, Ned."

Buchanan pretended to struggle with the command, but finally surrendered. "McDukes's word has always been his bridle. I'll go to my grave believing he headed to Scuffers Meadow intending to rid the world of Old Man Dekker, exactly as you ordered. His failure to rejoin us tells me he probably got caught and tossed in the pokey, much like they got you and me."

Buchanan was correct.

Juan Forminfante was at the root of McDukes's prolonged absence.

Forminfante recognized Swaney, the minute he saw him strut into the Scuffers Meadow jailhouse as bold as a slut's promise, calling himself Sheriff McDukes and seeking directions to Old Man Dekker's current whereabouts. He called the deputy to his cell, using stomach pains as his excuse. "That ain't no sheriff playing cute with you," he said. "No McDukes neither. His true name's Lowell Swaney, a wanted convict what escaped from Desert Prison, or my own rightful name ain't Juan Forminfante."

The deputy invited McDukes over and repeated Forminfante's words.

McDukes laughed at the notion. "I don't have no inkling about your prisoner. Never seen his face before now. No idea what makes him turn his lying tongue on me." He shook a clenched fist at Forminfante, who flinched.

"This situation calls for Old Man Dekker's wisdom to guide us to the truth," the deputy said. He pulled his Smith & Wesson on McDukes, relieved him of his weapons, and steered him to an empty cell. McDukes obliged without a fight, counting on his badge to outweigh whatever crime put Forminfante behind bars.

After the deputy left to find Dekker, Forminfante whistled for McDukes's attention. "Your name's Swaney, no matter who or why you call yourself otherwise. I was on the trail to find you, make myself some greenbacks, when this setback happened with the crazy man runs the town."

"Is there any more you care to share, maybe turn me into a believer?"

"More'n likely you'll get strung up before I have a chance at you and any reward money, so none's the harm," Forminfante said, and told him what transpired in New

Testament. "You manage to spring out from here before me, I'll eventually be back chasing after you and a crack at the promised reward."

The deputy returned with bad news. He said, "Our leader said to apologize, but he has pressing business to take care of first and will get back to you whenever he can."

"Why can't I be let out, promising to come back when Old Man Dekker is available?"

"He guessed you might ask that. He told me to quote from the Scuffers Meadow top twenty commandments, this being commandment eleven or twelve, he wasn't certain which: 'Thou shalt not for any reason, once in jail, be released without the leader's consent.' "

"He didn't consent?"

"He guessed you might ask that. He told me to tell you he can only consent for someone he meets in person and shares a true handshake with."

"Which commandment is that?"

"He wasn't certain. He said he's never been called on to use it before you."

Forminfante was unable to bring his laughing fit under control.

McDukes found nothing humorous about the situation. It got him wondering if Buchanan would guess the reason behind his absence if it lasted too long, use his gift of gab to get Jarman to order a charge into Scuffers Meadow. If anyone could do that, surely it would be Ned.

The day passed.

Then another.

And another.

McDukes filled the hours thinking back on what memories he was able to invoke. He was consumed by images of Flowing Beaver, surprisingly not of Jeanne d'Evreaux. Flowing Beaver was a hunger, where Jeanne was not even a recipe.

Both faded from his thoughts when Peg Terry came along.

Peg strolled up to the barred windows of his cell, unannounced, brash as cymbals, and said, "I hear tell you kill and do other awful things, but you hardly look the type."

McDukes was immediately captivated by her manner and beauty. "Tell me what you want to hear, for that's what I'll say if it keeps you smiling and in my sight, young lady." She lowered her wide hazel eyes and covered her mouth to hide her giggle. "Do I know you from somewhere other than this miserable jail cell? I sense I've known you a million years."

"I'm but nineteen, soon to turn twenty," she said, a lilt to her warm voice. "Besides, you silly man, nobody lives a million years."

"Meeting up with you is the same," he said. He only stared at her after that, fearful his words would drive the young miss from his sight.

She closed her smile and ran from the window, fearing, she would later confess, that he might understand her blush and hear the whoosh of her heart caused by the sight of him.

McDukes called after her, "You ain't told me your name."

If Peg heard him, she did not let on.

Not then.

CHAPTER 11

Peg returned often after that, always with fey excuses that disguised her true reason, her growing need to be in McDukes's presence. He disguised a similar need for her that he struggled to keep unspoken, given it was unhealthy considering the disparity in their ages.

One time Peg brought him a chocolate cake smothered in chocolate frosting and topped with a single candle, meant to observe their first meeting a month ago. The gesture both pleased and alarmed McDukes.

"I suppose there's a blade inside, sharp as all a tack," he said, thinking he'd made a joke.

It was no joke to Peg. She lowered her voice. "Yes, so don't let on where the deputy can hear us," she said. "I skinned the knife myself on my daddy's rig, tested the blade by halving an apple's skin. It's sure to help you escape from that hideous place."

McDukes told her to leave immediately with the cake, warning it could cause her serious damage if the blade were discovered by the deputy when she tried delivering it.

"Maybe he'd lock me up in the same cell as you. Would that be so bad? Not for me."

"Or maybe Old Man Dekker has a commandment for that. 'Thou shalt not assist in a prisoner escape under penalty of immediate death by firing squad.' I want you to be alive and breathing when he gets around to showing his face, recognizes a mistake's been made about me, and turns me out a free man."

"Eighteen."

"What?"

"His commandment. It's number eighteen, and it's death by fire, not a firing squad, the way it happened for Joan of Arc over the ocean in France when she was a mere twenty."

"Save the history lesson, sweet Peg, and do what I ask. Right now. For me."

"Anything for you," she said, and impulsively moved close enough to the window to reach him through the bars for a kiss that caught McDukes by surprise.

It was their first.

It seemed to last forever before he broke it off.

"Go on now. Git."

"That was nice," she said. "Can we do it again?"

"Next time. We'll do it again next time."

"*Next time.* The most beautiful words in all the whole entire world."

Years later, the dime weeklies described how Peg rushed home reveling in the kiss that exposed her secret love for McDukes. How she slept fitfully that night, excited by her need to visit him again tomorrow, share another kiss with him — maybe two or three or more — and how, maybe, McDukes might surprise her by revealing what loving feelings he felt for her.

Old Man Dekker had returned that same night and flashed a wanted poster with two sketches at McDukes. "You call yourself McDukes, where this shows you to be Swaney," he said. "I don't give a fiddler's bow which you are, seeing how the rewards are equal and fit for helping do God's work in Scuffers Meadow, so we'll be taking you back to Desert Prison come morning."

Peg arrived at the jailhouse in time to see McDukes being led away in handcuffs.

He spotted her looking distraught and

raining tears, trapped in a crowd assembled by Dekker to watch him exercise his authority. McDukes managed a smile and mimed: *I'll be back for you.* She answered in similar fashion as he passed her: *I'll be waiting.*

Fate dictated otherwise.

Her parents had had their fill of Old Man Dekker and his dictatorial ways after years of blind obedience. They decided to try their lives elsewhere, choosing a place they'd heard good things about, a growing town farther west called Tap Dance, her poppa explained. "The weather is fine year-round, the blue Pacific Ocean close enough to use for a washtub, and land available for any future I care to test," he said.

It was not the future Peg imagined for herself, but choice was out of her hands.

Once freed of prison, how would McDukes know where to find her?

When her parents retired for the night, Peg lit a candle and by its light wrote "Darling" in her graceful penmanship. No, not "Darling," she decided.

She began again on a fresh sheet of foolscap. "Dearest," she wrote, but was no happier. Were anyone to intercept her correspondence, "Dearest" would also expose her deepest feelings, something she was not yet ready to let happen.

"Mr. McDukes."

There.

Perfect.

"Mr. McDukes," she wrote: *"My poppa, momma, and I will shortly be leaving Scuffers Meadow, making tracks for someplace called Tap Dance. Do come and visit us for dinner when you are free of your prison sentence and in search of a fresh start among friends, for that is what we consider ourselves. I will bake a chocolate cake for dessert, if that appeals to you. Yours very truly, Peggy Elizabeth Terry."*

She posted the letter to him care of Desert Prison.

It never reached the real McDukes or Lowell Swaney, who was Peg's McDukes.

After she left the post office, one of Old Man Dekker's censors read the letter, decided it demeaned Scuffers Meadow, crumpled it into a ball, and tossed it away.

Not that it made a difference.

Desert Prison no longer existed, destroyed in a series of raids by Soaring Eagle, the demon of the Plains.

Peg's "Mr. McDukes" was being taken by train, under guard, to Fort James Emerson Ford Federal Prison.

McDukes, in actuality Swaney, cuffed to his

window seat, entertained himself on the long ride by studying the passing scenery.

He watched assorted creatures of the desert, envious of their freedom, wishing he were one of them, even the Gila monster or the mosquito or the fire ant or the spider or the snake or any one of those tiny black specs of insect he couldn't name that competed for life in a world outside their control.

He saw cattle being led to slaughter or milling about in circles, providing a break for the longhorn cowpunchers grown weary on the grassy trails. He saw nomadic Injuns traveling alone or in small bands, on the hunt for buffalo and safe shelter. He saw caravans of settlers heading in either direction, intent on settling down someplace new that offered them a better future for their families.

Ronnie John, the guard seated across from Swaney, was an easygoing, talkative fellow in his deeply wrinkled sixties, cultivating a long white beard that reached his bay window and was meant to make up for his total lack of hair topside. He was never short on stories about his life and work, and laughed himself to tears at his bottomless chest of hoary jokes.

Swaney had to pretend sleep to avoid his

company. That didn't always work. Ronnie John would tap him for attention whenever he needed to use the gent's or find a porter or the candy butcher to replenish his supply of cream cigars, candy rolls, and jelly beans.

"Don't go anywhere before I get back," he'd tell Swaney, as if that were an option.

Returning, it was always, "Happy to see you're still here," punctuated by a giant laugh, but not this latest time.

"I just saw me a beaut," Ronnie John said, puffing on a fresh stogie.

Swaney said, "Meaning what, Ronnie John?" making conversation to take the edge off his boredom. "I don't suppose you mean some elegant stallion running wild."

"Hardly, although I've seen horses like that," he said. "This time, for as many times as I've made the ride, there's been none so pretty as this fine young lady, mighty big of belly and looking to foal soon,"

"Sounds like a woman I could like for myself," Swaney said.

Ronnie John choked on his laugh. "You could not qualify to smell this woman's fart. There's no way I can describe the sensation that ran through me when I sighted her. Everything about her was special, lacking only me in her company. You? Never."

"I'd like to observe this remarkable female

for myself," Swaney said, waving away the smoke from Ronnie John's cigar. "Spring me free of the cuffs and I promise to return after making my own judgment."

Ronnie John reared back in his seat and shook his head. "Try me on that request when pigs can fly, Swaney. Use the present and your future time at Fort James Emerson Ford Federal Prison to cultivate memories of some woman already in your life, assuming one exists."

Swaney retreated into himself, eyes shut, manufacturing images of Flowing Beaver and Peg Terry, uncertain which one he cared for more, unaware the woman on the train Ronnie John spoke of was a lost memory from his forgotten past —

Jeanne d'Evreaux.

It became a question of survival after the hell-raising cowboys left Swaney for dead and took off with Jeanne. They robbed banks for sheer enjoyment as well as profit, they told her, and she was welcome to join in the fun or die an ugly death after all of them tired of taking multiple turns between her shapely limbs.

Jeanne chose a robber's role, not because she feared death or being used for their sexual pleasure, but for the sake of her unborn child. From the start she proved good at it, came to enjoy it, and even took the lead on multiple occasions.

She dressed in a fabric shirt, ordinary pants, and leggings, wore a bandana to hide her face, and favored a heavy coat to disguise her condition, easily passing for one of the boys. Her pistol was ever at the ready, and she sometimes hoisted a shotgun, ready to use either weapon, but hoping it would never come to that. Her one distinguishing feature was her French accent, which led the dime weeklies to label her "The Frenchman." Their circulation rose any time the cover illustrations featured her and the stories chronicled her daring deeds, most of them editorial inventions.

The cowboys came to call her "Frenchy," gave her the type of respect reserved for the best in any profession before their attempt to rob the First Bank of Trepidation turned sour. The bank was on alert for them and had Pinkerton agents armed and ready to shoot to kill when the robbers rushed through the front door and shouted their demands.

In the brief gun battle that ensued, the cowboy leader and most of his gang were killed.

The few who retreated shouldered a

gravely wounded Jeanne.

She was bleeding profusely and scarcely conscious.

Her condition slowed them down and endangered their escape.

They left her behind to die on the dirt road.

The first to reach Jeanne was a bank customer who had been drawn into the battle, Dr. Marion Wilson Beverage.

Dr. Beverage had served with distinction in the military, attaining the rank of captain before his retirement, and was no stranger to the sight of blood.

"This one's still breathing," he called out. "Need help getting him to my office."

It wasn't until he had Jeanne stretched out on his operating table that Dr. Beverage realized his patient was a woman.

He applied all his skills to saving her life and nursing her back to health in the weeks that followed, saving her from arrest and trial by supporting and enlarging upon the claim she was the gang's prisoner, unwillingly brought into their nefarious undertakings.

In the process, drawn closer by her luminous beauty and the history she shared with him, the good doctor fell in love with Jeanne, so deep and strong, it's unlikely he'd have been upset to discover her true past as a whore or that she'd invented a dear, devoted, loving, now-deceased husband to explain the baby in her belly.

"How did he come to leave you, your husband?" Dr. Beverage asked Jeanne once she was fully recovered.

She assigned blame to the bank robbers. They murdered Pierre when he defended her virtue, she said. She broke into tears describing that horrible day, and begged Dr. Beverage to drop the subject.

He reached for his Bible and read her some of his favorite passages, inviting her to read along with him. She welcomed the opportunity to please him and made a game of their reading together. The doctor would speak first in English and she would repeat the passages in French.

After a time, he took to marking special chapters and verses for her attention. Sometimes, the Bible markings were made prior to Jeanne's bedtime. Other times, they were there when she woke in the morning.

One morning she was surprised to find him in her bedroom, frozen in place a few feet away, staring at her with bug-eyed admiration, uncertain what to do next.

"Join me," she said, patting the bed.

"You're sure about this?"

"*Oui.* I have wanted this with you for the longest time." It wasn't the truth, of course, but it was something Jeanne felt she owed him.

Dr. Beverage disrobed and crawled under the covers with her. "My way with women is very limited," he said.

"Then I will show you what I know, *mon chèri.*"

Afterward, they spent an hour praying together.

Her lesson turned into a nightly ritual, always followed by a Bible reading, a prayer, and, frequently, a sermon on the values and virtues of an honest life, until the time came he could no longer contain himself and blurted out his love for her.

"I wish to marry, if you will have me," Dr. Beverage said, shaking with fear she might reject him. "I wish to take on your unborn child as my own, as his natural father. I wish to leave Trepidation and create a fresh life for the three of us someplace where we are not known and you will not be haunted by your criminal past."

"You would do all this for me?" she said.

"For the three of us, Jeanne."

Jeanne understood she owed her life to the pious doctor, but was less certain she cared to become his wife. Was the future he

131

pictured even close to the one she used to see in her dreams? Images of Swaney and McDukes, even Cactus Billy Clemens, clouded her mind and added to her indecision.

She sensed he would not leave without an answer and, after all, she could always change her mind and disappear into the night. "Then *oui, merci,* Dr. Beverage. I am happy to accept your proposal."

The doctor allowed no time for Jeanne to change her mind. He whipped out the diamond engagement ring he had been carrying for weeks and slipped it on her finger. She welcomed his embrace and kiss with believable warmth and affection.

"What is this new place you talk of for our new life, Dr. Beverage?"

"Have you heard of the township named Tap Dance?"

"Non," she said. Why any truth now? It would only lead to questions she would decline to answer honestly.

"It's a virgin land almost as far west as the ocean," he said. "It's a place where old lives can end and new lives can begin, ours as well as the child coming."

The description he painted moved her to genuine tears, and in that moment she came to feel for him the way fools feel for one another, but her sense of unbridled happiness only lasted until the morning, when a Pinkerton called on them.

Dr. Beverage met him at the door, recognized him for what he was by the "Sunday best" suit, bowler hat, and bow tie all the Pinkertons favored, along with a neat handlebar mustache and the overpowering smell of lilac cologne.

He showed identification and said, "We recently were informed one of the outlaws we bested at the First Bank of Trepidation, whose life was saved by you, is a woman, none other than the notorious 'Frenchman.' Correct?"

"Jeanne d'Evreaux, but not one of the outlaws. A captive they forced into service and since absolved of any guilt by the good people of this town."

"There are others elsewhere who may not feel as generous, sir. I've been warranted by the government to take her into custody for transport to their jurisdiction, where she will get a fair and just hearing."

"Miss d'Evreaux is still under my care here and not fit for travel."

"With all due respect, get her, so that I can judge her condition for myself, please."

"Certainly. Come in and be comfortable in the parlor while I fetch her."

Dr. Beverage returned within minutes. He was alone.

"Miss d'Evreaux is dressing and will join us momentarily," he said.

He continued to advance on the Pinkerton until close enough to plunge a scalpel into his neck, puncturing the carotid artery. The Pinkerton, caught off-guard, could not stop the blood flow.

Dr. Beverage watched him die.

"It's safe to come out now, sweetheart," he called to Jeanne. "We must hurry. We have much cleaning up to do before we can safely begin our journey to Tap Dance."

Swaney's reverie was interrupted by train robbers who entered their coach with demands for enough money and valuables to fill the hat one of them would be passing down and around. "Don't disappoint us if'n y'all know what's best foh y'all," their leader said, wigwagging his Colt .45 revolver for emphasis.

He was a granite-faced fellow of average height in his late twenties, his accent straight out of Dixie; eyes dead behind an iron stare; mouth locked in an uninviting expression; brown hair growing thick and tall atop a broad forehead.

Swaney called, "You're James, Jesse James."

James smiled at hearing his name and stepped over. "How do y'all come to know me, the magazines that chronicle my exploits?"

"Them an' your picture decorating every post office in the land. You are one famous lad, Dingus."

"What's your story?" James said, pointing at the handcuffs.

"Been on some of the same walls and currently riding under armed guard to Fort James Emerson Ford Federal Prison, unless you might be of a mind to help me out of my predicament and these damn shackles."

"This gentleman, he your guard?"

"Yes, sir, Mr. James. Ronnie John's the name an' surely a pleasure to meet you."

"Then you won't mind freeing my friend, will you, Ronnie John?"

"Truly sorry, Mr. James, but I can't do that. I'm duty bound by law to keep him in my custody until I turn him over to the authorities at the fort."

"Guess I got no choice but to remedy that," James said, and shot the guard, causing a hole in his chest big enough for a baby possum to pass through.

Passengers in the coach reacted with

shock and fell silent, fearing any one of them might be next.

Swaney studied the lifeless body of Ronnie John slumped over in his seat and marveled to himself at the cruel casualness James displayed dispensing sudden death.

James directed one of his men to search the guard's body for his weapon and the keys that would free Swaney.

He had Ronnie John's gun handed over to Swaney and said, "I'd welcome y'all to enlist in our merry band of Robbin' Hoodlums, but we're short on mounts, so best y'all hop off when there's a slowdown round a bend, and good luck. There's danger lurking out there from Injuns on the warpath. Meanest critters y'all ever seen."

They shook hands and Swaney stepped outside the coach onto the open platform to wait for a curve. He jumped clear of the train when it arrived, but rolled out of control down a steep ravine, crashing into boulders all the way to the bottom, suffering a series of hard knocks to the head that left him unconscious for hours.

Finally rousing, he had no idea where he was or how he got here, except for a vague memory of riding the rails.

The pain and the bruises added a jumble of names and memories, foremost among them at first a girl named Peg Something, who mistakenly called him McDukes, where anybody who knew him knew him as Lowell Swaney, the name he owned since birth.

McDukes, damn his ornery hide. Where was he now?

And Ned Buchanan?

And the woman soon to mother his child, Jeanne d'Evreaux?

He was aiming Jeanne for a better life where he owned acres, a town way west called Tap Dance, when a band of badass cowboys took them prisoner, put hungry eyes on her before they beat him senseless, and —

What did they do with Jeanne, those merciless sons of bitches?

Where was she now?

That's as far as the thought took him before vague images of an Injun girl traveled in and out of focus.

What was that all about?

And who else, Swaney?

What else, Swaney?

Everything else was a blur beyond value.

Maybe sleep would help him to clear his mind.

He woke hours later to a rustling in the brush and found himself staring back at a half-dozen redskins, their bows and arrows aimed at him, bloodlust burning in their eyes.

CHAPTER 12

While Swaney now knew who he was, the legitimate McDukes was not as fortunate.

The circumstances that kept him believing he was Lowell Swaney would soon deliver him to Fort James Emerson Ford Federal Prison.

His problem began when the legit McDukes, Ruben Garner, and Little Tad Logan escaped capture after holding off Colonel Francis Milstead Keepers's gunslingers in the gaming parlor ordeal that lasted more than a week.

The dime magazines chronicled various versions of the siege.

Most favored the colonel's, in which he painted himself a hero.

On the rare occasions Garner was quoted, he spoke otherwise. "We got away clean after nine days, sneaking off in the dark of night, so that makes Keepers a loser the way I read it," he said. "Even offered a lift to this gal we found was hiding in our midst, nervous as all get-out and afraid the next round of bullets might claim her. She declined, saying nine days gone from home and no fresh knickers would be hard enough to explain to her husband."

He kept that to himself. Earlier and he might not have dallied with her those several times they used a break in the attack to secret themselves in a far corner and dally away, always instigated by her, claiming it would calm her nerves and quiet her fears. Garner was too polite to resist her needs and play Good Samaritan.

In Ned Buntline's earliest recounting, he wrote of a cessation of gunfire that inspired the notion to chance escape among McDukes, Garner, and Logan. Their assumption was correct. The colonel had called a halt to the attack, fearing further destruction to the gaming parlor, which he owned, would destroy its resale value.

He dismissed his men with orders to stand by for any alert and returned home.

Crept into bed and nudged his wife.

She wasn't asleep, but making a good show of it.

"Did you miss me after so much time away?" he said.

"Yes," the colonel's wife said, "and I know you missed me."

Some hours later, McDukes, Garner, and Logan stopped to rest their mounts, refill their canteens with fresh water from a shallow creek, and decide where to head. "It's yonder for me," McDukes said, pointing out a direction. "Got a feeling in my bones it'll lead me to the Injun girl I seek an' a miserable snake in the grass what got her with him, name of Pronto Leaukomia."

"No, siree, not me," Little Tad Logan said, with a furious resolve the other two had not experienced before. "Apologies, McDukes, but I got me better to do when it comes to rescuing some redskin, no matter in whose company."

Garner also backed off joining McDukes. "I got my own unfinished business taking me in another direction," he said. "Logan, I'm up for a helping hand if that suits you more to your liking."

"Redskins?"

"None by choice."

"Suits me fine," Logan said.

It wasn't long after he and Rube Garner vowed eternal friendship and parted company with McDukes that all of Colonel Keepers's men who took part in the gaming parlor gunfight were shot dead under mysterious circumstances by a gunslinger who was never identified.

The colonel was the lone exception.

Squeaky floorboards roused him and his wife from their contented sleep by the masked intruder aiming a Peacemaker. The colonel sat up, supposing a gunshot any second would be the last sound on earth he'd hear. His wife pulled the blankets over her and started praying through her tears.

Her reaction caused the intruder to walk around to her side of the bed and yank the blankets down for a better look at the colonel's woman. He recognized her at once from their gaming parlor dalliance, and answered the plea for mercy in her liquid gray eyes by tossing the covers back over her and leaving.

The killer was never found, and not even the colonel could explain who or what was behind the attacks, or so he said. He offered a simple explanation for why he and his wife were spared a similar fate.

"When that coward looked at me, ready to end our days, he saw no sign of fear in my eyes, only the same unyielding hero's stare that came to distinguish Francis Milstead Keepers from any other colonel protecting the good citizens of this great country."

Meanwhile, as this happened, the real McDukes, still believing himself Swaney, fell into the company of a master rogue named Harvey Whiting.

Whiting was a graduate of the Bunco game, an acknowledged master of Eight Dice Cloth, an artist when it came to crooked lotteries offering spurious rare books and painting masterpieces as prizes, and a variety of other illegal pursuits.

In sum, he was bad news, but not to look at him.

Whiting's handsome face, musical voice, and polite manner, as well as his inexpensive business suit and string tie, often reminded people of a favorite schoolteacher or preacher, two roles among many that he played to the fullest when called for by the con, like the one he was running when McDukes came across him and a sick boy he identified as his son by the side of the trail.

The boy, not yet into his teens, was shedding giant tears and suffering an out of control hacking cough.

"You are the first rider to pass this way since my child fell too sick to travel," Whiting said. "Is it too bold to ask you to stay here and watch over him while I ride to town and fetch a doctor?"

"And I should believe you why, Harvey Whiting?"

Whiting was surprised to hear his name called out. He said, "How do you come to know me, stranger?"

"Yer reputation is well known for the scheme dealer you are, Whiting, and I even saw you doing your Bunco specialty once or twice in towns we both happened to visit the same time. This game is new on me, and shame on you for dragging in some kid and passing him off as your own."

"He is mine, and his sad condition is real. I've been using it as cause for travelers to stop and inquire. They do, I draw my .45, relieve them of their valuables, and send them on their way. Been making out like a bandit, changing locations on a regular basis until he turned worse than ever, as bad as you see him now."

"That so, sonny?"

The boy responded by coughing his lungs clean and spitting phlegm on the ground.

"Is that a satisfactory answer?" Whiting said.

"Better than if you tried drawing on me, which would leave you dead as a doornail before your gun was halfway out your holster, that's how quick I am. You stick here. I'll ride into town and come back with a doc fast as possible."

"You'd do that for me?"

"For the boy, not fer you, Whiting. What's the nearest town?"

"Heads High."

"Never heard of no Heads High."

"Then you'll be lost before you ever find it," Whiting said. "How about you stay with my boy and I'll ride after the doctor?"

"How can I trust you to return?"

"I'm leaving him in your care, that's how. Henry, you good with being left in the care of this stranger?"

The boy coughed loud and clear, clouding the air with spit.

An hour passed, then another, most of a third before Whiting returned, accompanied by three men wearing badges and aiming shotguns at him. Their leader said, "I wouldn't make no false moves I was you, McDukes."

"Name's Swaney, not McDukes."

"Says you, but not the wanted post prominent in my office. Either way you're a wanted man and Mr. Whiting here collects his reward money whether you go gently with me and my deputies or hang deceased over your horse. You choose the former, we take you back to Heads High first, then off to Fort James Emerson Ford Federal Prison."

"How about Judas? He goes scot-free?"

"Got nothin' to charge him with, except for bein' a stand-up citizen."

Whiting said, "Sorry, McDukes, but I recognized you at once from seeing you in action in another town some years back. I had to do my duty and bring our chance meeting today to the attention of Sheriff Arnett."

"What about the doctor for your son?"

"Henry, you in need of a doctor?"

"No, sir. Just a touch of the flu is all. Feeling better already."

Heads High was situated between two tall towers of solid rock, in a narrow canyon only wide enough for a single avenue of commerce bordered by one- and two-story wood structures thrown up when gold fever brought hundreds to the region, all hungering for their share of the mother lode.

There were newcomers among the failed veterans who traveled from one strike to another living on a dream that panned out only sometimes and, of course, there were

146

the scarlet women available day and night.

Flowing Beaver came to be among them, brought to Heads High by Pronto Leaukomia, who took her as his prisoner after losing sight of Colonel Francis Milstead Keepers or hopes of claiming a reward by capturing Swaney and McDukes.

Flowing Beaver seemed the only bargain left to him as they followed a shortcut running parallel to the heavily traveled Difficult Bends route, growling at her multiple times, "I'll find me other ways to profit off'n you, you ugly squaw mucker."

She chose a night when the moon was in full eclipse to attempt an escape, but didn't get far before Leaukomia woke, realized she was gone, and chased her down.

He overpowered her, dragged her to their campsite, and used his belt to strap two layers of skin from her back, until he had exacted her promise not to try running again and to obey his every command.

Not fully satisfied, Leaukomia beat her until she begged him for permission to obey.

Beat her again, until Flowing Beaver was incapable of begging.

Through it all, she framed her mind on a day when she would take command, when he would least suspect what she planned to have him long remember, when she would see to it he came to envy eunuchs.

On the night before they reached Heads High, she managed to pull Leaukomia's Bowie from his saddlebag and charged at him while he was engaged stirring a kettle of rabbit stew over the open campfire.

Alerted by the snap of a twig, Leaukomia sprang up, grabbed her by the wrist, and wrested the Bowie from her grip. He smacked her dizzy and threw her onto the ground.

"I need to learn you a lesson, you redskin savage," he said.

He used the blade to cut off one of her pinky toes and forced Flowing Beaver to watch while he sucked the toe dry and swallowed it before getting back to working on his rabbit stew.

She knew to prevent infection by applying taproot and wrapping the injured area in rag strips. Come morning, she was able to limp into Heads High behind Leaukomia.

He found the town's house of pleasure and traded Flowing Beaver for a tidy sum of cash, Madam Sophie delighted to add a redskin with a missing pinky toe to her stable.

"I been needing some new leg-spreader who'd have erotic appeal for my twisted regulars," she said. "You brought Flaming

148

Beaver to me at the perfect time, Pronto."

"Flowing Beaver."

"Not anymore. *Flaming* Beaver promises the chance for greater thrills, so I'll have them paying more nuggets and dust for the pleasure of her company."

"I should have bargained for more money."

"Both pinky toes missing, maybe a big toe, you might have had cause."

Heading from town, Leaukomia was called by a drunk who seemed incapable of crawling his way out of a mud puddle. "Pronto, surely you remember your old sidekick, Laredo? Fallen on hard times, I have. What say you toss me a coin or two for old times' sake?"

Leaukomia tossed him a dirty look instead and continued on, deaf to the insults Laredo was screaming at him in two languages.

Madam Sophie knew her business.

Flowing Beaver became a much in demand treat for customers who happily forked over a premium price to play with the missing pinky toe, around which the madam concocted elaborate, raunchy stories that tweaked their imagination and got their juices flowing; never the same story twice.

Flowing Beaver rarely talked about the toe.

She rarely talked at all.

She painted Leaukomia on the walls of her eyes and her memory. She burned his image into her mind. She prayed to her gods to keep him safe and from harm against the day she would see him again, the day she would smile again. She would take control of him, take her revenge through "duhmett," which in the language of her tribe meant "a sight defying sound" to some, "everything from nothing" to others.

She was taken by surprise the day a white man new to her bed pointed to the absent toe and said, "Duhmett, Flaming Beaver? Revenge, maybe? I don't know what ails you, but I can cure it for sure, if it's a cure you're after, and I can return your toe if the payment justifies the reward."

Duhmett?

Her toe restored?

Few outsiders were versed in the ways of her tribe.

What made this paleface different?

Curiosity took held of her.

"Duhmett, toe," she said, breaking her silence. "What you want for this?"

"You tell me," said Harvey Whiting, who lately was calling himself "Harvey Winslow."

He had learned early in the confidence game, while mastering his craft, that it always was better to have the mark make the buy rather than him the sale.

Flowing Beaver grew silent again, unsure what of value she had to offer. "Got no money. Madam keep it all."

"Something else, maybe? I'm open to suggestions."

"One thing, maybe."

She wriggled out from under Winslow and went after the papers Secret Sun had given her for safekeeping. She had hidden them before from Leaukomia and now from Madam Sophie, in the back of her dresser drawer, tied by a ribbon and covered by stained undergarments.

Blinded by the prospect of this white man restoring her toe, hoping Secret Sun would understand when once more fate brought them together, she handed over the packet to Winslow.

He examined the papers with growing delight —

Deeds to land and lots of it in a place called Tap Dance.

The name was new to him, but he knew the value of valid deeds of title.

They meant easy money, if not by ownership, by the profit to be made passing them

151

on to a gullible taker he would charm with visions of a golden future. In any event, the deeds would do him more good than this gullible Injun trapped in bondage, with scant hope of ever regaining her freedom or her missing toe.

"I'm a fool for accepting this, but I do it out of compassion for you," Winslow said. He passed a hand over the maimed foot. "Listen for the sound," he said, tightening his britches and his smile. "It will mean the toe is on its journey back to your foot, and you can ready yourself for the vengeance you seek."

"How long?"

"Patience is called for, child. Do not lose faith, for that can cause the greater powers to abandon your claim."

Her heart was brimming with happiness when Winslow left.

She shed tears of joy.

This white man was no Pronto Leauko-mia.

This white man was a friend with magic powers.

All thanks to Harvey Winslow, she would have her pinky toe back.

She would once again walk erect, without the limp.

Days passed.

She waited patiently for her toe to arrive.

Anxiety brought on sleepless nights.

She turned indifferent to her work, causing regulars and newcomers alike to complain to Madam Sophie and demand their payment returned. The disgruntled madam threatened to take the whip to Flowing Beaver if she did not snap out of her funk, or explain what had brought it on in the first place.

Flowing Beaver explained everything.

"You stupid redskin whore," Madam Sophie said. She slapped her hard across one cheek and then the other. "He played you for the fool. Your toe ain't coming back and neither is he."

Flowing Beaver flopped on the bed and hid her face in shame, unable to decide who was the greater pirate, Pronto Leaukomia, who took her toe, or Harvey Winslow, who took her mind.

Harvey Winslow fled Heads High before the truth could catch up with him.

Now calling himself Herbert Whiting, he moved on to Pentameter, a town he sensed was ripe for the pickings.

The population mainly comprised gandy dancers, snowshed guards, stone carvers, steel hammerers, and others who built mighty railroads to run like plows and cultivate the crops of culture from one coast to the other. Only their appetite for play matched their thirst for work and life itself.

In this they were often joined by loggers, who came from the nearby forests in ox-drawn wagons, their muscles aching for the grease of rotgut whiskey.

Whiting settled in after a quick survey to make sure no one knew him.

This included Ned Buchanan, a mainstay at the many watering holes dotting Main Street, all of them busy to overflowing twenty-four hours a day.

They met for the first time soon after Whiting chose as his next mark Miss Ada Clokke, a stage performer who had traveled west with her company of ladies, "Miss Ada Clokke and Her Tick-Tock Review," to provide evenings of entertainment at reasonable prices.

There were thirty ladies in all, most American and British, three Orientals, one colored. They sang, danced, played instruments, and performed comedy skits for two hours, including one encore.

Whiting caught up with Miss Ada Clokke during rehearsals at McHugh's Mighty Music Hall, which in the past had drawn full houses for veteran artists like Southern,

Drew, Booth, Foy, and even the Jersey Lillie herself. He charmed her into giving them a few minutes alone and used the time to tell her a story made of whole cloth.

"Dear lady, word is quietly spreading among promoters that you and your most talented troupe have failed to attract audiences and turn a profit for them wherever you have performed to date. Consequently, a meager audience at your first show in Pentameter will result in the balance of your engagement being cancelled."

Miss Ada Clokke found the news jarring. Her mouth dropped open in silent dismay and she clutched her ample chest. "So not true," she said. "We have played to full houses from the onset of our first tour away from our home in Chicago, Illinois."

"Then perhaps I misunderstood what I was hearing, although I did hear it from a source as reliable as sunrise and sunset."

"Mr. McHugh? If so, I will seek him out immediately and correct his invalid impression."

"I'm not at liberty to say, but I will urge you not to do so. He hates confrontation of any kind and might fire you on the spot. I believe a wiser course of action would be to do whatever it takes to make certain you fill every seat in the music hall."

Her legs failed her; she sank onto a chair. "Such an effort is beyond my knowledge and capability."

"Not as difficult as you imagine, Miss Ada. I've done it many a time myself."

"I don't suppose you'd dare do it for me?"

There!

He had hooked her.

Now to reel her in.

Whiting said, "I was about to move on, having completed my business here, but I have never been one to abandon a damsel in distress. I would be honored to serve you and the ladies of your theatrical company, see to it every seat in the music hall fills, give you an audience generous in its appreciation and applause for the abundance of talent and beauty you exhibit on the stage."

"You would do that?"

"As sure as my name is Herbert Whiting, 'Herbie' to my friends, but buying goodwill is a costly enterprise, and I lack sufficient funds to sustain such an undertaking."

"How costly?"

Whiting didn't rush into naming an amount.

"Please, Mr. Whiting, Herbie — I'm asking how much?"

"Maybe you'd be better off simply chanc-

156

ing what happens, for better or for worse."

"I have my mind set on you, Herbie. How much?"

Whiting threw up his hands and threw out an amount.

"Agreed," Miss Ada Clokke said. "That sum will erase what profit the company has turned to date, but it is a sound investment in our success here and our future on the road."

Whiting roamed among the hard-drinking denizens of the Pentameter bars, offering them one by one what he described in a whisper as the chance to purchase participation in the special show that would follow the opening night performance of Miss Ada Clokke and Her Tick-Tock Review at Mc-Hugh's Mighty Music Hall.

They handed over gladly the astronomical sum Whiting quoted once he defined the cast as women of free spirit, who disguised themselves as stage nymphs in order to elude the scrutiny of the law and probable arrest.

Their purchase bought the railroaders and loggers more than normal stage entertainment, Whiting clucked and winked. More than singing. More than dancing. More than dramatic and comedy skits and recitations. They would be free to stage a show of their own, satisfy the outer limits of their imagination.

Opening night.

The music hall was packed to almost twice capacity.

The show started promptly on time. Heavy applause, whistles, and cheers greeted the opening song of welcome sung by Miss Ada, a dancing chorus of cast members behind her. Enthusiasm diminished as time passed and the drinking progressed nonstop.

The audience grew restless and noisier by the minute. After an hour, the catcalls were louder than any applause and there was a growing demand for the special performance they had bought and paid for. "Ain't waiting no more for after the show," a muscle-bound logger said, his voice sloshing the declaration. He hopped onto the stage, grabbed onto an Oriental, threw her to the hardwood, pounced on top of her, and called out, "Timber!"

That served as a signal for all of Whiting's duped customers.

They attacked the stage and the women, getting full value for their investment by putting sex and violence on drunken display.

Herbert Whiting was gone by then, nowhere to be found.

He was on his way to the horse barn to grab his mount and head elsewhere even before the curtain rose on Miss Ada Clokke and Her Tick-Tock Review, where he came across Ned Buchanan, asleep on a bed of hay in one of the stalls.

He found the itch to make another score before leaving town was irresistible.

He squatted beside Buchanan, turned his head away from the heavy stench of whiskey breath, and nudged him awake.

"I'm Henry Whippet, sir, and, although a stranger to you, I pray you might be inclined to grant me the favor of hearing my situation."

"Huh?"

Henry adopted a gloomy expression and put a choke in his throat. "I'm racing off to join my aged mother in an effort to save her from losing her home to bankers intending to toss her to the street for her inability to meet her mortgage obligation any longer."

"Good luck an' kill all the bankers is what I say."

"Good luck will not save this day, sir. It's hard cash money they are insisting upon."

"Kill 'em all, anyway, says me, an' all the attorneys while you're at it."

"You strike me as a gentleman blessed

with generous intention, sir. Perhaps you have a thought or two about how I might save my widowed Momma from an indignity likely to kill her?"

"Won big at the blackjack tables, I did. What if I loan you what you need to save the dear woman?"

"You would do that for a complete stranger?"

"I'd do that for anybody what's in need." He fumbled a thick role of greenbacks out from his jacket, counted off several hundred dollars, and handed over the bills. "How's that?"

Whiting saw Buchanan still had a roll the size of a billiard ball. He was overtaken by greed. "Generous, sir, but far short of what it will take to satisfy those greedy bastards."

"Kill 'em all."

"If you were able to part with more, rather than a loan, I am prepared to sign over to you ownership of land leases worth far, far more than my poor Mama's immediate need. Look here." Whiting held out the papers. "They are for treasured acreage near the Pacific shore, by a town called Tap Dance."

Something Whiting said struck a familiar chord.

Not his name; *Henry Whippet* was new to

Buchanan.

Tap Dance, that name.

And *land leases,* that sounded familiar, too — too familiar.

Buchanan tried recalling why through his bourbon haze.

Impulsively, he grabbed the papers away from Whippet and subjected them to closer inspection. "I seen them before," he said, suddenly sounding less drunk as his whole demeanor turned urgent and dangerous. He drew his Peacemaker and aimed it at Whiting's gut. "Tell me where you got them papers from or draw your final breath, your choice."

Whiting became a coward's best advertisement.

He told his story swift and clean, investing most of the truth with a few omissions.

"You say an Injun whore?" Buchanan stared ominously at Whiting. "What else? What of Swaney and McDukes? You know them names?"

"No."

Buchanan pushed the Colt hard into Whiting's gut.

Whiting's memory improved at once. He owned up to having crossed trails not long ago with a cowpoke calling himself Swaney, but looked more like the McDukes portrayed in wanted posters.

When Whiting ran out of recollection, Buchanan demanded return of his money and, in turn, shoved the lease papers back at him. "I got no use for land and less for you who'd invent a mother in distress to support his crooked ways. I know your face now, Henry Whippet. I'll be coming after you for certain if what you had to tell about Swaney and McDukes turns out to have me chasing after the wild goose."

Without so much as a backward look, Ned Buchanan saddled his horse and rode off for the town of Lonely Vigil, where Swaney or McDukes might be jailed, stopping first at the town of Heads High for a whorehouse visit with an Injun who walked one toe short.

Heads High no longer existed.

The town had been reduced to a pile of rocks.

No survivors, Buchanan thought, until Heck Jarman and Lonely Todd Logan materialized from somewhere in the dusty rubble. "The earth shook and the mountain come down, turning the town into a graveyard for them wasn't fast enough to get out from under," Jarman said. "Me and what few's left of my boys are headin' off for parts unknown. You're welcome to tag along if you're of a mind, Ned."

"I'm on my way to Lonely Vigil, if that trail appeals to you and the others, Heck."

"Not so much for me, old friend, so this is goodbye, again for now."

Lonely Todd Logan spoke up for the first time. "Think I'd like to stick with Buchanan and try Lonely Vigil, you don't mind, Heck."

"A lonely gent for a lonely town. Why not? Nothin' to mind, Logan, but I will miss your company."

They shook hands all around, and Buchanan and Logan took off together.

Their second night on the trail, Buchanan suffered a bad dream bordering on a nightmare.

In the dream, Buchanan was chasing an Injun whore who limped, yet was too fast for him to catch.

She turned a dark corner.

He followed after her.

She was gone, disappeared, replaced by a disembodied voice informing Buchanan there would be no Swaney for him to locate in Lonely Vigil. There would be no McDukes.

Buchanan demanded: *Where are they gone to? Where will I find them?*

The voice's answer jarred him awake.

He waited for daylight to tell Logan, "We got us a new destination, so pack up and let's get a move on."

"Where might that be, Ned, or is it a secret?"

"Fort James Emerson Ford Federal Prison," Buchanan said. "That's where we'll find Swaney and McDukes."

"And you know this how?"

"Heard it firsthand from a ghost."

Chapter 13

Warden Chester "Cap" Yokum knew his prisoner wasn't Lowell Swaney, certain he was McDukes, having been acquainted with both during his military years. He liked them until they quit liking each other over some business about McDukes's dead wife. Now, the best he could muster toward the one standing across from him in his office was indifference.

"You are not Lowell Swaney," Yokum said, and let it go at that, without bothering to explain he recognized him as McDukes.

"You're wrong as a mud hen's final hoot," said McDukes, still believing he was Swaney.

"No difference anymore. They pay me by the numbers I watch over, not the names. If it's a Swaney they want under lock and key, it's a Swaney they got."

Yokum's guards also were indifferent, except when it came to wagering over who would control the prisoners, the same kind of betting pool that existed at Desert Prison, where Swaney once held sway and achieved legendary status by defeating Bill "The Butcher" Barton and Grief Bonner.

The symbol of power here was not a fruit tree, but a giant boulder that dominated the Fort James Emerson Ford Federal Prison courtyard.

McDukes, even with memories of Frank Maelstrom fresh in his mind, had no interest in serving the guards' betting pool by taking on the reigning Boulder Boss, as proposed to him by the lead guard.

"I ain't here to fight," McDukes said. "I'm here to serve out my time, that's all."

"Suit yourself," the lead guard said, "but be prepared to suffer the consequences." He offered a Derringer to McDukes, who declined the gift. "Another mistake, Swaney, one you'll regret when the Boulder Boss comes after you, for that is how the game is played inside these walls."

"The way I know it from experience, carrying a firearm is an invitation to trouble, and I already got my share of trouble."

"Not yet around James Emerson Ford you don't," the lead guard said. He brought down the Derringer on McDukes, which dropped him to the ground, then added

166

several nasty kicks. "Being armed and attacking a guard, that's going to cost you time to reflect in the shithole, Swaney."

McDukes wasn't alone during his time in solitary confinement.

He shared the cell with a mouse, already there when McDukes arrived and looking happy to have company. McDukes, similarly pleased, found he could translate the mouse's squeaks into words.

Their chats were amiable and inconsequential, a way to pass the hours, until somebody tossed a warning note through the security window of the heavy iron door. He shared it with the mouse: *I are the Boulder Boss and not you ever, so watch it when you out from there and don't try nothing. Otto Grass.*

"What are you going to do about it?" the mouse squeaked.

McDukes balled the paper and flushed it down the toilet.

"Got to face up to reality, Mouse. Doin' something goes against my grain, but doing nothing is worse two ways from Sunday. It'd get guards kicking me down here regular-like until I change my ways and the prisoners branding me a coward for steering clear of the Boulder Boss, Otto Grass."

167

"Can you take Grass in a fair fight?"

"Fair or otherwise, I got no memory of ever losing and would not aim to make this the first time, Mouse."

McDukes bid a sorrowful goodbye to the mouse a few days later, when they returned him to the general population, unaware the mouse had somehow managed to trail after him. He stuck to his cell until he felt free of the recurring double vision and other problems he attributed to the beating he had taken.

Word spread rapidly when he began a soldier's march to the big boulder, a toothbrush parked under his shirt, its handle sharpened to a fine point.

Wagers were still being made when he arrived.

The convicts were betting their money, smokes, and other items of commerce on Otto Grass. They feared Grass and were comfortable having him as their Boulder Boss. The guards were united behind Swaney, especially those aware he was actually McDukes and enjoyed a winner's reputation on both sides of the law.

A half-dozen inmates were hanging out around the boulder.

McDukes stopped a yard or two away. "Which one of you gents would be Otto

168

Grass?" he said.

A bald-headed, heavyset giant stepped forward. "That would be me," he said in a thick foreign accent McDukes took to be German. "What name is it you go by?" Pretending like he didn't know. Fat lips pulled back in a wide-mouth smile showing missing teeth, gold molars, and purple gums.

"The name's Swaney."

"Yah, thought so. You look like I was hearing. Up until now I thought, maybe, you were hiding away from me and the fate awaiting you if you ignored the warning I sent. You come try and take the big boulder for your own anyway? A fool's mission."

"I ain't no fool, Otto."

"Tell me so after I kill you dead."

"I'm thinking otherwise, but first —"McDukes held up a bottle of toilet bowl hooch he had found stashed under his bunk by the cell's previous tenant — "I figured we share a friendly drink before I send you down to Hell, Otto."

"Hah, hah, hah, you are some jokester you are, but why not?" Grass stepped forward, accepted the bottle from McDukes, and swilled more than half before handing it back. "What goes good right now, a fine cigar, but I have only one, so sorry for my rudeness." He retrieved the stogie from a shirt pocket and popped it between his lips.

"No offense taken, seeing as how it'll be your last stogie ever, Otto."

Grass laughed and frisked himself unsuccessfully for a match.

McDukes had some smokes and wooden stick matches on him.

He snap-lit a match with his thumb and held it out for Grass.

A light breeze sailing through the yard caught the flame, joined it to the hooch residue on Grass's lips and teeth, and sent it with lightning speed down his gullet to his lungs and belly. He howled in pain before his vocal chords fried and his insides turned to toast, already a dead man beyond rescue.

It was an accident, but most of the guards and convicts figured it was a devilish killing designed by Swaney, who was now automatically Grass's successor as Boulder Boss, welcome to carry the title until someone came along to challenge him and win.

Back in his cell, McDukes said, "I need to set them straight on that score, Mouse. I been clear how I don't want to be boss, any boss, especially under false pretenses, and they should go get someone else."

"You keep the truth to yourself, you know

170

what's smart for you," the mouse said. "You let on Otto Grass found his own way to die, the betting pool will be a mess, what with refunds being demanded, and new enemies looking to own your scalp."

McDukes tried the logic as his own on Warden Yokum, who bought into it without a moment's hesitation. "Solid thinking, McDukes."

"Swaney."

"Yes, fine. Solid thinking, Swaney. Anyone dumb enough to take you on, we both know he'll get his comeuppance, maybe even worse than Otto Grass. Stay in line, do your time, you'll be gone from here like it was the day before tomorrow."

As the dime weeklies always noted, good advice has its exceptions.

The one here was called Ross Bullion, but he was only a nameless shadow the night he sneaked unseen into McDukes's cell, wielding a length of lead pipe stolen from the laundry and set on revenging the death of his close friend, Otto.

It was not yet three o'clock, McDukes sound asleep and cultivating a loud snore.

Everything was average about Bullion except his murderous intent. His first swing with the pipe caught McDukes at the base of the skull, the next on the side of his head.

171

The third blow ruined his shoulder. The one after that, the last one, came down on his ribs. Satisfied McDukes would be dead by morning, Bullion slipped out of the cell and disappeared as quietly as he had arrived.

McDukes survived, confirming history's later verdict that he was too damn tough to die on any basis but his own. He spent weeks recovering in the prison infirmary, under heavy guard against further attacks; in a coma, and unaware of frequent visits by his friend the mouse and by the warden, who was at his bedside the day he opened his eyes for the first time and struggled to make his words understood.

"Where I at? How I get here?" he said.

Warden Yokum told him.

"Who did to me?"

"We haven't found him yet, so until we do I'm having you kept under 'round-the-clock protection, with a bunkmate for added security."

"Okay," McDukes said, suddenly more concerned with remembering his past.

The blows to the head, instead of killing him, had given him back his life before darkness stole it and led him behind bars at Fort James Emerson Ford Federal Prison.

Not all of his memory, not yet anyway.

Names were slowly fitting into place like

pieces in a complex jigsaw puzzle, and events no faster. First to come to mind was Ellie, his wife, then Lowell Swaney, whom he blamed for Ellie's death and had sworn to kill in return. Jeanne d'Evreaux, the whore both he and Swaney coveted for reasons still unclear. He thought of her next. And Ned Buchanan and Lonely Todd Logan and Cactus Billy Clemens and Colonel Francis Milstead Keepers and who else? Denny Slime and Juan Forminfante. An Injun girl and —

and —

and —

McDukes fell back to sleep.

The bunkmate was waiting for him in their cell the day the prison doctor ruled McDukes healthy enough to leave the infirmary. He was a cowpuncher of average everything, nothing to make him stand out in a crowd, but there was a certain familiarity about him.

"Names Bullion," Ross Bullion said.

"No, sir, the name's McDukes," McDukes said, and shook Bullion's hand.

"You mean Swaney, don't you?"

"If I meant Swaney I would of said it. We ever met before this?"

"No. I was in the yard the day you took

173

on Otto Grass and turned him into fireworks to inherit the big boulder and become the Boulder Boss. Might that be it?"

"Could be. I'll think on it and let you know. For now, go on and tell me what you know 'bout the big boulder and this Grass fella and how I got almost dead and whatever else that's all about."

Bullion obliged the request.

"So, I'm hearing right, you volunteered to put yourself in the line of fire to help protect me against any new tries on my life." Bullion's head bobbed up and down. "Makes you one brave cowpuncher in my book, nothing I would of guessed."

Bullion, so the stories go, sought out Cherub Flannery, whose baby face disguised the black heart of a born killer. Flannery fed his taste for blood in the service of other convicts, in particular those who showed respect for the professional quality of his work. The guards gave him free reign and distance as payback for the work he sometimes did on their behalf.

Bullion took Flannery aside in the courtyard, checked for privacy, and said, "Cherub, my good friend, I've been wondering of late why you never became the Boulder Boss."

174

"No interest, Ross, especially not if I had to go up against old Otto, a good man who took to the title like it was his true measure. Me? My good name and reputation is all the title I need."

"You know about the new Boulder Boss, name of McDukes, who faced off with Otto and got him measured for a coffin?"

"Old news. You telling me you got some beef with this McDukes needs mending?"

"Not that, Cherub. Hear me out. The warden has me sharing a cell with him since he was attacked and almost killed by someone after checking out of sick bay."

"By who?"

"It's a guessing game so far, but McDukes talks in his sleep and I heard him calling out your name more than once."

"Me? He's insane."

"I think so, too, but I wanted you to know, and also the rest of it."

"What rest of it?"

"I heard him saying: 'Cherub Flannery, you would face me in broad daylight if you were a real man of courage, not a coward who waited until I was asleep before launching your attack on me.' "

"A coward, he said of me? This McDukes has another thing coming, Ross. You tell him that for me. Tell him he's about to come up against a real man of courage first thing tomorrow."

Bullion said, "You sure that's a good idea, Cherub?"

"Could be the worst idea in the whole damn world, but nobody gets away with calling me a coward," Flannery said, and tramped off muttering angrily under his breath.

Bullion waited until the recreation hour passed and the convicts were herded back to their cells before raising the subject with McDukes.

"Why's he coming after me tomorrow, what's that about?" McDukes said.

"He says he's been hearing from people you're going around accusing him for the attack on you and calling him a coward."

"No such thing. Ain't been accusing anyone, much less Cherub Flannery. You tell him that?"

"I tried, but he wouldn't hear me out. His mind's made up; set in stone."

"Tomorrow it is then." McDukes unleashed a giant sigh. "What's it about prison can turn people loco? Stir crazy, I think they call it. More and more I been thinking I need to get out of this place while the getting is good."

Bullion slept well that night, satisfied he

176

had created a situation that would bring about the revenge on McDukes he sought, this time without the need to filthy his own hands.

In the morning he told McDukes: "You go ahead and I'll catch up."

McDukes did fifteen minutes of warm-up exercises, parked his toothbrush in a pocket, and headed for the courtyard and his face-off with Flannery at the big boulder.

A mixed crowd of convicts and guards was already assembled.

Betting was brisk, the odds favoring Flannery by a small percentage.

A cheer exploded when Flannery showed up across the yard about twenty minutes after McDukes.

Flannery balled his fists, raised his arms to signal victory, and let out a bull-like roar before he charged at McDukes, maintaining a steady aim with a Derringer he pulled out from inside his waistband. He fired on the run and missed.

McDukes stepped aside as Flannery reached him and, with the skill of a matador, plunged the sharpened handle of his toothbrush into Flannery's neck.

Blood spurted from the wound.

Flannery dropped the Derringer, then

grabbed onto McDukes to keep from falling.

McDukes stabbed him again, this time between the shoulder blades.

Flannery refused to let go.

"Don't you ever again go calling me coward," he said.

"Didn't ever in the first place, Flannery. What give you that far-fetched idea?"

"Bullion, he told it true to me," Flannery said, and died in McDukes's arms.

By now, the convicts and guards had closed in on them, all united in singing praise for McDukes, chanting his name, hailing him as a most worthy Boulder Boss.

Bullion was the first to arrive, his smile as wide as the Mississippi. "I thought I saw him saying something to you before he was done for. Anything important?"

"No," McDukes said, doing his best to look like he meant it, his mind made up to deal with Bullion's deceit before he got other business out of the way, like figuring how to break out of this crazy house once and for all.

To hear the dime weeklies tell it, that's how matters stood before redskins took to the warpath and headed for Fort James Emerson Ford Federal Prison, led by Soaring

Eagle, the warrior chief responsible for the bloody massacre at Desert Prison.

CHAPTER 14

Soaring Eagle was the last of the wilderness warriors, the worst of the lot, with a manic desire for a final revenge. He wanted the palefaces to learn and remember that Sitting Bull wasn't the only warrior who spoke for the red man. "I intend for my voice to be heard, to speak for history," the dime weeklies quoted him as saying in translation, and maybe he did.

He meant the total destruction of Fort James Emerson Ford Federal Prison to be his final achievement, Buntline and others wrote. To Soaring Eagle, it was more than someplace to store criminals. It was still a fort, the dishonest government's last one, a holdout against the roads and rails of changing cultures, a reminder of the shame his people had suffered.

"I will kill this fort of iron bars and show the white intruders how we will ride forever, one hand on the kingfisher and the other

180

on the coupstick," he said. "I will lead the charge and claim the answer to sun-dance dolls and sleeping bears on the summit of shaman's tort or gahe dancers' antics."

To make his vision clear, he killed a berdache and dared the berdache to kill him back.

Or something like that.

Soaring Eagle did not intend to blindly lead his warriors into battle.

He dispatched Walks Like a Duck, the former Rachel Stump, a fair-skinned captive since her teen years and now the oldest of his seven wives, ahead on a spy mission. Walks Like a Duck had come to love him and obey his every wish. Suitably clothed, she presented herself at the fort as a nurse separated from her wagon train in the aftermath of a blinding sandstorm.

Warden Yokum welcomed her warmly, saying the fort could always use a good nurse, especially during the prison riots season, which occurred seven months out of every year, often longer. She regularly strolled the grounds memorizing the weakest walls, crawl holes, and other avenues of access that would help her beloved Soaring Eagle gain his greatest triumph.

Once she had accumulated all the information he would require, she took a pony out for a ride and never returned.

The warden took her disappearance philosophically. He wrote in his diary: *I suppose too much work for the young lady is what drove Nurse Stump away. I'm sure going to miss her, that pony even more.*

When the war party came into sight, the first warning was sounded by a tower guard who understood the significance of the dust clouds drawing closer.

McDukes, now whole in the head, owner of the courtyard boulder, and still sharing a cell with treacherous Ross Bullion, rushed to join the tower guard and see for himself.

He recognized the Injun leading the charge by the number of palm leaves painted on his brawny chest. They told how many battles the chief had won on horseback and in hand-to-hand combat.

The chief was most certainly the dreaded first among warriors, Soaring Eagle.

Behind him was a force twice the size of the entire prison population, armed with bows and carbines, their war bonnets boasting many bird feathers, each one awarded for bravery in an earlier skirmish.

Warden Yokum arrived at the tower, took aim with his spyglass, and was unhappy with what he saw. "The bows worry me more than the carbines," he said. "A bow sends arrows more than one hundred yards with damning accuracy. The arrows find their mark faster than any rifle or single-shot Colt or Remington. And see there, McDukes. They got knives for close combat and taking victory scalps, like they did at Desert Prison. It surely don't look promising for us."

The guard fell to his knees and prayed.

"A miracle would be nice about now, but we can't count on one," the warden said. "The cavalry is way too far away to come riding to our rescue; the sky too blue, the sun shining too warm and bright, for us to expect a rainstorm that would discourage those bloodthirsty savages."

The guard prayed louder.

The Injuns stopped advancing, as if the guard's prayer had reached them.

In fact, Lowell Swaney was responsible.

He had caught up with the war party and raced forward to catch Soaring Eagle before he could start the battle by dancing the pole of hawk feathers and hurling sacred truths at Acapona, the mighty god of war.

Sitting tall, wearing the magic headband of Noku, the mighty god of truth, that protected him from harm, Swaney conversed with Soaring Eagle in the tribal sign language taught him by the chief's captive wife, Walks Like a Duck, the former Rachel Stump.

"I humbly ask you to forget this war for now and invoke the name of Corvis, your mighty god of good deeds."

"That is Drago. Corvis is our mighty god of good hunting, under which you were caught. Drago is the reason you still live, that and because of a plea by Walks Like a Duck that I granted, rarely able to deny her any wish."

"Drago then."

"Why? What is it that moves you to this request?"

"A convict of my close acquaintance that I have called friend for many years, McDukes by name. I wish to see him to safety."

"Tell me then, did you make this request of Prodge, our mighty god of friendship? You would need this done before turning to Drago."

"I admit I did not do so in my haste to reach you."

"I welcome your good sense and, recognizing you are new to our customs and language, invoke Nort, our mighty god of understanding and forgiveness. I will turn back home with my braves so you might rescue your friend, but it is only a temporary departure, so be swift about it."

"Why not forever, Soaring Eagle? Haven't you proven your greatness by now?" Swaney said, tapping the magic headband of Noku.

Soaring Eagle raised his voice in anger. "You will be wise not to challenge my wisdom again, white man. Destroying this fort will set my place among the great leaders. It will set my place in history. It will set my mind at ease with my soul. Only when this happens will I retire from war and take up the peaceful pleasures of farm life."

He moved fingers over fingers, index in and palm to half circle, thumbs aloft; then extended his arms and clamped his hands to the sides of his head, anchored by his middle fingers. "Go after this McDukes. On that you have my agreement. After that, go far away. Don't return to my sight, or it will be your death along with all the others."

"How much time you giving me?"

"Until I hear again from Acapona, our mighty god of war."

Soaring Eagle steered his mount around and signaled his braves to follow him back to their encampment, leaving Swaney to find his way inside the prison walls to break out McDukes.

Swaney slept that night under a blanket of stars and a cacophony of sounds from prairie animals and insects, thankful to still be alive, remembering the circumstances leading up to this time.

He was certain he was a dead man when the redskins came upon him, but they tied him up and took him home with them to impress Soaring Eagle with their hunting prowess. Soaring Eagle was on the verge of ordering him burned at the stake as a sacrifice to Lakintabrohah, the mighty god of death and dismemberment, when a sweet-tempered voice called out, "Let him live, my dearest darling love."

This was Rachel Stump, Soaring Eagle's seventh wife, the only white woman among them.

"Why should I spare him, Walks Like a Duck?" he said, puzzled by an interest she had never before shown toward any captive.

"He can satisfy my growing desire to learn what history I've missed since falling away from the white man's world and into your warm and welcoming arms, allow me to practice my English tongue before it fades entirely from memory, and maybe even teach him our language in exchange. Is that asking too much of you? If so, I will be the one to put the torch to the stake."

"Not ever do you ask too much of me," Soaring Eagle said. "You may keep your new toy until you tire of him."

Swaney learned there was another reason when he and Walks Like a Duck were alone in his teepee.

Walks Like a Duck said, "I heard you calling yourself by the name Swaney when you first were brought here. Is that so? You are Swaney?"

"As sure as you didn't start off a squaw. What matter does my name make?"

"And you know a man calling himself McDukes?"

Swaney recoiled at hearing McDukes's name erupt from between her lips. "How do you come by knowing that?"

"He spoke of you while recovering from injuries at Fort James Emerson Ford Federal Prison."

"You heard McDukes say this in his own words?"

"I was inside the prison, as if I were still a nurse called Rachel Stump by name, but, in truth, to spy for my dear Soaring Eagle before he leads the attack that destroys the prison and all within its gated walls, includ-

187

ing your friend."

"Why are you telling me this?"

"McDukes said to me one time, almost in jest, to give you a message if we ever crossed paths, to say he still has you and somebody called Ellie on his mind. So there you are, Swaney. Now pay attention while I begin teaching you our hand talk."

Thoughts of McDukes clouded Swaney's mind afterward. McDukes not so long ago had busted him out of prison. Swaney owed him. It was Swaney's turn to return the favor, but how? It was nothing he had to figure out immediately. McDukes wasn't going anywhere soon.

Swaney settled into Injun life, never losing sight of his goal.

Weeks passed by, one day like the next, until a morning when he woke to an unusual stillness. He discovered why wandering the camp.

Only the squaws, their children, and the ancients were there, going about their usual business. Soaring Eagle and his braves were gone.

Swaney found Walks Like a Duck, who said, "They left dressed, armed, and painted for battle at Fort James Emerson Ford Federal Prison after Acapona, our mighty god of war, spoke to my beloved."

188

Swaney rode off at gallop to catch up to Soaring Eagle, hoping he was not too late.

"Who goes there, friend or foe?" a boyish, freckle-faced guard at the prison entrance said, taking steady aim at Swaney with his Springfield carbine.

"Both, so take your pick. Name's Lowell Swaney, a wanted man, an' I just come here from turning back a bunch-a Injuns bent on owning your scalp. You need to get me to your boss pronto."

"You expected? Warden Yokum got strict rules against people wanting his valuable time without first getting an official appointment."

"How do I do that?"

"I don't know for sure. This is a first time for me."

"Let's go and ask Warden Yokum."

The guard considered Swaney's suggestion. He nodded approvingly. "I like that idea. C'mon in."

Warden Yokum was in his office with McDukes, plotting proper defense measures were the Injuns to return. McDukes seemed an unlikely choice to anyone unaware he had served in the military and was an expert on battle strategy, or so the dime weeklies portrayed him.

He recognized Swaney at once, but Swaney's eyes and tightly drawn lips signaled him to keep it their secret.

The warden said, "Does this cowboy have an appointment, Jarman?" The guard shook his head. "Then why is he here?"

"Says he's a wanted man, sir."

"No appointment, he's not wanted by me. You know the rules, Jarman. Sorry, cowboy. Come back when you have an appointment."

McDukes said, "Slow down, Warden. If them Injuns return, we're going to need all the manpower we can muster."

"Good thinking, McDukes. Cowboy, how do you feel about facing off with savage Injuns on the warpath?"

"Wouldn't be the first time, Warden. Besides, I been living with this tribe and I'm the one got them to turn around and leave you be the last time they was here. It won't happen like that again, so you need to be ready to take them on."

"You know how?"

"I got ideas."

The warden slammed a palm on the desk and pointed a finger at Swaney. "It was you McDukes and I watched do that — that's why you look downright familiar. Right, McDukes?"

"Couldn't agree more," McDukes said.

"What's your name, cowboy?"

"Swaney. Lowell Swaney."

"Okay, Swaney. Pull up a chair. You got yourself an appointment. Good work, Jarman. You're excused."

The warden was all bluster when Swaney made enlisting all the convicts in the prison's army of defense part of the plan, an idea promptly supported by McDukes.

"Insanity," he said. "Not all can be trusted, some among them who'd sooner slit my throat as leave it to the redskins."

"It's a necessary gamble," Swaney said. "You're far outnumbered otherwise to have even a fighting chance at coming out the winner when they show up wearing their war paint."

"They don't come back, I still got a problem on my hands."

McDukes said, "I'm the Boulder Boss. I say the word, your convicts won't dare come up against me, Warden, and you know you got me on your side."

Warden Yokum cracked a smile. "McDukes here, he's very loyal."

"And never wrong," McDukes said, taken immediately by Swaney as a reference to

191

the ongoing vendetta of his making about Ellie.

"Everyone's good for at least one mistake in his lifetime," Swaney said, and changed the subject back to the impending attack. "What do you have by way of weapons, Warden?"

"Hundreds of sabers. An equal number of twenty-inch bayonets that rig on to our single-shot. Breech-loading Springfields. Also a supply of the lighter, shorter Springfield carbines, but sadly no repeating Spencers, a seventh bullet part of its standard load, which I favor, although the Springfield is more accurate at longer distances."

"Ya sound like a military man what knows his way around arms," Swaney said.

The warden beamed. "Cavalry officer, rank of captain, with the Frontier Brilliants, under the command of Colonel Francis Milstead Keepers. You know that name, of course."

Swaney and McDukes exchanged looks, but said nothing.

The warden wasn't through retreating into memory. "We won our boldest headlines and brightest medals after destroying the redskin village of Whadduss, under direct orders of General Jamboree John Jackson. I still hear him clear as day telling the colonel within my earshot: 'They are Injuns, and that's reason enough to eradicate the lot.'

"Colonel Keepers wondered about the women and the children.

" 'I said the lot, large and small alike, Colonel.'

" 'The children then?'

" 'Nits make lice,' the general said.

" 'There are some who will brand you a heartless fiend, General.'

" 'And others who will urge me to run for Congress, Colonel Keepers. I hope you plan to land on the right side of the coin.'

" 'Anything less would be insubordination, General.' "

Frank Leslie's dime magazine was the first to report the story in full detail, explaining how the colonel directed his aide-de-camp, Captain Yokum, to fill the men with ample whiskey and women the night before the raid. Come morning, the Frontier Brilliants rode off to do battle at the Wadduss village some distance from their own camp.

The village was unguarded and believed by the tribe to be safe from attack under a government treaty that gave them full title to the land and guaranteed peaceful coexistence.

The men were away hunting, days removed from the carnage to come.

Left behind as usual were the women, their children, and their respected elders.

Many of the troopers questioned continuing the assault under those circumstances, but were too hung-over to disobey Colonel Keepers's unflinching order to continue or risk courts-martial and imprisonment on grounds of insubordination.

An ancient was the first to see the Frontier Brilliants charging and shouted: "Stop now! Now! Now stop!" in a language they didn't understand and had no intention of obliging. They rode him under.

The air clogged with the sound of fired pistols, Springfields and Spencers; the screams of the dead and the dying.

A squaw sent her young son forward waving the white flag of truce. A soldier's bullet struck the boy dead. The soldier leaped off his mount. Hooting with joy, he took the boy's scalp.

Another soldier killed and scalped the boy's mother.

Others used toddlers for target practice.

Colonel Keepers smashed an infant against a tree, inspiring similar deeds.

The squaws were raped, some multiple times, before their throats were slit.

The massacre didn't stop until the troopers had no one left to kill.

They returned to camp with wet scalps hanging from belts and bayonets, in total silence where earlier they had been a choir of joyful noises as they caused bodies to fall and blood to be shed. Mostly sober now, they recognized the enormity of their unnecessary deed.

General Jamboree John Jackson remained jubilant, calling the event a warning to any Injuns who had it in mind to challenge the white man's way, little expecting his words to be taken as a challenge and inspire a passion for revenge that led to the destruction of Desert Prison.

Warden Yokum turned away from Swaney and McDukes. He recognized the look on their faces and what they now must be thinking of him. "You got it wrong if you think I was party to that horror," he said. "I was there for certain, but removed myself from the charge and fired not one single shot. I killed no one, but I live with a memory that has scarred me forever."

"You could have stopped the horror before it began, Warden."

"How, Swaney?"

"Kill the general if he refused to rescind

the order; the colonel, if he tried stopping you."

"That would have been treason of the worst kind and probably have me hanging from a rope. Instead, I got a commendation in my jacket and landed this job after putting my uniform in mothballs." He changed the subject. "So, if as you propose, I turn my convicts into fighting men, what then, Swaney?"

"While they're guarding the fort, McDukes and me, we make our way to Soaring Eagle's camp. We find Soaring Eagle and kill him on the spot. Without a leader, there'll be no attack and you're back to normal here."

"You believe this scheme of yours will work, Swaney?"

"Who lies for the privilege of spitting into a volcano, Warden?"

"I'm game," McDukes said. "I got nothing to lose but my life."

"What guarantee do I have that you'll come back, McDukes?"

"The Injuns don't kill me first, I need to finish up my sentence and leave prison a free man."

That was less than the truth, of course.

McDukes saw Swaney's plan as an opportunity, finally, to kill him in revenge for the death of Ellie, and blame his murder on Injuns.

The warden wandered the office, hands locked behind his back, lost in serious thought with himself. "Okay, then," he said, finally. "Let's do it."

The next day, sometime after midnight, Swaney and McDukes were packed and ready to head after Soaring Eagle, using the cover of darkness to sneak in and out of the Injun camp.

The warden, who had busied himself training the convicts, showed up unexpectedly.

The two armed convicts with him had their Springfields leveled at Swaney.

"Swaney, I am hereby relieving you of your freedom," the warden said. He showed him a wanted poster. "This caught my eye late in the day, after staring me in the face all along. You're a wanted man, Swaney, a big bounty on your head, so I'm not about to risk you taking off and never showing up again around these parts."

"If that was my intent, what was I doing here in the first place, except to try saving your prison and everybody from Soaring Eagle's bloody intentions?"

"You tell me."

"What I will tell you — you all are facing

war for certain if you all don't let the plan go forward."

"The plan is definitely going forward, only not with you."

McDukes, silent until now, said, "Respectfully, if you expect me to take it on alone, you got another thing coming, Warden."

"Give me some credit, McDukes. You won't be alone. I've chosen a candidate to replace Swaney, who swore he's up for a dangerous mission, especially alongside the Boulder Boss — your cellmate, Ross Bullion."

Bullion chose that moment to materialize in the doorway. His smile hid his pleasure at being handed the unexpected opportunity to kill McDukes as payback for killing Otto Grass and afterward flee to freedom.

"A fine choice," McDukes said, invisibly overjoyed by the chance to repay Bullion for his treachery and afterward, back at the prison, blame the Injuns before figuring out how best to kill Swaney.

Why McDukes and Bullion would be leaving the fort, to kill Soaring Eagle, seemed of little or no importance to either man.

"Hear me out, Warden — you are making a big mistake not letting me go," Swaney said, before Warden Yokum had him led away to solitary confinement. "Without my guiding hand, they'll be captured by Soaring Eagle an' his Injuns an' die a horrible death before the moon rises one more time."

"You sure are full of yourself," the warden said, and let it go at that.

CHAPTER 15

Ross Bullion struck first.

He and McDukes had set up a temporary viewing post within sight of the tribe's camp, taking turns with the spyglass, watching for some sign of Soaring Eagle.

Just as the orange glow of day peeked over the horizon line and the camp began stirring with activity, Bullion pointed and said, "I just spotted him coming out of that teepee yonder. He matches the description Swaney gave you. See for yourself." He handed over the spyglass.

McDukes studied the scene hard. "I don't see no one who looks like that," he said, his last words before Bullion crashed a heavy rock on the back of his head.

McDukes slumped over.

Blood seeped out from the crack in his skull, discoloring the sandy turf.

Bullion studied his handiwork. "And that's that," he said, approvingly. "Otto, my dear friend, revenge has never tasted sweeter than it does this here moment."

He didn't have more than another minute to enjoy it.

Gravel cracked under soft footsteps.

Turning, Bullion found himself facing a trio of armed braves, one with a bow and arrow, the other two with pistols. He understood at once he no longer had something to smile about.

Soaring Eagle materialized after Bullion had been staked to the ground. He wasn't alone. Standing by him was a face Bullion recognized, Rachel Stump, the nurse who'd come and gone from the prison, only now she had traded her uniform for a squaw's dress.

The chief did some mumbo-jumbo with his hands.

Rachel Trump translated. "My dear husband wishes to know if you have any last words before you are sent off to join your ancestors."

"I mean him and his tribe no harm, Rachel."

"Walks Like a Duck is my true name." She repeated his answer in sign language. Soaring Eagle responded in kind. "My dear husband says Corvis, our mighty god of good hunting, came during the night to warn him otherwise."

"Corvis was mistaken."

"My dear husband says you are the mistaken one. He says Corvis is never mistaken."

Soaring Eagle turned and left, leaving Walks Like a Duck to follow in his tracks.

The squaws stepped forward to begin their work with a tanning, indifferent to Bullion's screams and pleas for mercy. They chattered among themselves, using their long blades with a skill born over years of practice to cut open his belly and remove his entrails. They compiled thin slices of meat that would be left to dry into jerky for the lean months, when buffalo meat was in short supply. They pulverized fatty flesh and blended it with wild berries to create the strength-giving treat called "pemmican."

Their work done, the squaws stepped aside, allowing warriors to dance around Bullion's carcass, their hair unbraided, chanting songs of victory that became part of their culture after the white devils first arrived to claim ownership of the land.

It was McDukes's turn next, but tribal custom and practice called for him to be whole of body and spirit. The ceremony would have to wait until his head wounds had sufficiently healed. So would Soaring

Eagle's attack on Fort James Emerson Ford Federal Prison, taking the chief's frustration to the breaking point.

He gathered his council of elders for an emergency powwow, then presented his belief that the capture of the two white devils signaled that the fort was readying for battle.

"We cannot allow them to gain any advantage this might give them over us. We must strike now, before more time passes," he said.

Fleet of Feet, the oldest of the elders at one hundred and two years of age and slow of speech, said, "On this do you have concurrence from Acapona, our mighty god of war?"

"I have not heard from him as of yet, learned elder."

"From any of our mighty gods?"

"Or them, learned elder."

"Then you have no choice but to wait, Soaring Eagle, for that has been the unbroken rule among our people for as long as I can remember." He managed to his feet without assistance. "I must go and make pee-pee now," he said, and left the council chamber one careful step after the next.

The other elders followed Fleet of Feet out, marking the first loss Soaring Eagle ever suffered at their hands. Feeling abandoned by the gods, his anger past its limit, he called for Walks Like a Duck.

She came running, all smiles, unaware what he had in store for her, as if this turn of events was all her fault.

"Yes, love of my life, what may I do for you?" she said.

The day passed, then another, giving the lie to Swaney's prophecy about when to expect an attack, Warden Yokum decided. To be certain, he returned to the guard tower and surveyed the land with care.

No sign of Injuns.

Not so much as dust clouds a charge would cause.

He was satisfied McDukes and Bullion had accomplished their mission.

Did success cost them their lives or had they taken sweet freedom as their reward?

He didn't care which.

They were heroes.

They deserved medals for saving the fort from destruction.

And, by the way, he had Swaney in solitary confinement, a wanted criminal with a bounty on his head. Under other circumstances, Swaney would also deserve a medal, for his words of warning that set the plan against Soaring Eagle in motion, but criminals deserved prison, not acclaim.

Maybe he should visit Swaney and thank him for his contribution.

That struck him as the right thing a commanding officer would do with subordinates. He'd observed it done before by Colonel Keepers and even General Jackson.

The warden climbed down from the tower and headed across the yard to the bank of solitary cells.

Swaney's cell was empty.

He was gone.

A thorough search of the fort came up empty.

Swaney's escape in the middle of the night was the doing of Ned Buchanan.

Buchanan had entered the cell without making a sound and startled Swaney awake by clamping a hand over his mouth. At first Swaney thought it was somebody out to kill him, but knew better when he heard Buchanan's familiar voice saying, "Just follow me, Lowell. We can talk once we're long gone outside the walls of this hell hole."

"Tell me first how you got in here, Ned."

"Same way I'll be getting us out. I bribed a guard with a tall stack of greenbacks, like I did once before getting you and McDukes out of Desert Prison. Greed recognizes no borders."

Swaney said, "Need to take a friend with us."

"What's that about?"

"This little critter here." He nudged the mouse sleeping alongside the bunk. "Hey, you, little feller. Wake up. We're on our way to freedom and I wouldn't think of leaving you behind."

The mouse's squeaks sounded more like squawks before he lapsed into silence and shut his eyes again.

"Mouse wished us safe journey, but he ain't coming along. Says he's been in here too long a time to consider being anywhere else."

Buchanan eyed Swaney suspiciously. "You actually talk to that mouse?"

"Talked to lots of rats in my time, so why not a mouse?"

Two hours later, sharing coffee, brandy, and conversation by an open fire, Buchanan said, "Long time for us together since you took your leave from Jarman and his gang, Lowell."

"Long time," Swaney said, no idea who Buchanan meant by "Jarman," but of no mind to ask. He said, "Tell me, Ned — how's it you come to know I was at Ford

Prison and showed up to spring me free?"

"Matter of fact, I was there after McDukes. Couldn't find him anywhere I checked, but there you were in solitary, snoring loud and clear on a worn-out mattress thin as a pancake."

"You got a destination in mind?"

"General direction of Casa Pleach."

"Never heard of the place."

"Neither has the law."

Sunrise, two days later.

Soaring Eagle gathered his warriors and led them on the warpath to Fort James Emerson Ford Federal Prison.

So determined was he to have his revenge on the white devils, he had lied to the council of elders, swearing by Noku, the mighty god of truth, that Acapona, the mighty god of war, had answered his prayers and given him permission.

As dime weeklies forever after described the ensuing massacre —

The Injuns climbed past walls and battered down doorways along a route Walks Like a Duck had fashioned while acting as nurse Rachel Stump.

The entire population of the fort, taken by surprise, surrendered without incident.

Soaring Eagle had dictated no prisoners,

except for Warden Yokum, and the wholesale slaughter began. The initial cries rising from guards and convicts alike had them begging to be allowed to live. As the Injun cruelties accelerated, they pleaded for pity and a faster death.

According to Leslie's magazine, the warden sought to hide in a storage basement, but was found balled up like an unborn child and delivered to Soaring Eagle. The chief threw him into a cell and left him with a ration of pemmican, a ration of jerky, and a half-filled canteen of water before padlocking the door.

The warden, sweating fear and inevitability, said, "Have you no decency, you redskin son-of-a-bitch? You don't know me. You don't play fair. Kill me and be done with it."

"I know you for what you are," Soaring Eagle said, his English better than anyone might suspect. "I remember you from when you and your blue britches rained death upon my village. I lived by lying still among the dead and the dying, swearing an oath to Lakintabrohah, our mighty god of death and dismemberment, that I would seek revenge."

"I killed no one that day. I was an innocent observer."

"No one there was innocent that day,"

Soaring Eagle said, and left, ignoring Warden Yokum's pleas for mercy.

The fort was torched, the flames and the smoke rising high into the sky. Soaring Eagle and his warriors, singing tribal songs of victory, headed away, unaware they had left behind a mouse deep into mourning the loss of friends.

Not long afterward they were on the run from a special military regiment assigned by the president himself to seek and destroy the perpetrators by any means necessary. Almost a year later, Soaring Eagle was cornered like a bastard mutt in a remote area of Canada by a corporal, said by Ned Buntline's dime weekly to have lost kin in the Ford Prison massacre.

The corporal secured Soaring Eagle to a chair and punctured him time and again with his bayonet, drawing more and more blood. He worked from the bottom up, saving the Injun's eyes for last, so the Injun could see as well as feel the pain he was inflicting.

Soaring Eagle presented a brave front until the pain was unbearable.

"Enough, please," he said. "Let me go, my friend. You have proven your point. I am here to be a farmer and nothing more."

The corporal took his left eye first.

McDukes awoke the day of the massacre, fully recovered from Bullion's blows.

He was alone.

He peeked outside the teepee door to confirm what his gut was telling him — only squaws and old men were around; Soaring Eagle had left with his warriors to attack the fort.

This was his chance to escape before they returned.

He dressed, found his mustang, and rode off without attracting notice.

Not far gone on the trail taking him to Casa Pleach, McDukes heard moaning in the tall sagebrush that lined the grimy trail and stopped to investigate.

The noisemaker was Rachel Stump.

She had been beaten, mutilated, and left for dead.

"Who did this to you?" he said, feeding her water from his canteen.

Too wounded to understand the question, she struggled to speak. "Not there, my dear husband." She managed a scream. "Not there, please, my dear husband. No, no, no, no, no." Another scream.

"The favor would be to leave you here to

die, but I can't do that," McDukes said, "Not as long as there's a breath of life sticking to you that suggests you might survive."

He lifted her up with care and strapped her slung over the backside of his mustang.

They traveled like that for days, Rachel Stump no better or worse than the day he found her, McDukes desperate to reach someone or someplace where she could get better care than he could give her.

The trapper who stepped out from behind a tree was not the help he needed, as evidenced by the shotgun he aimed at McDukes.

"I'll be wanting your valuables," he said, "including them furs you got bundled back there on your horse."

"What you see as furs is a lady dying if she don't get medical attention, and this ain't helping the cause any, mister."

"Then you best hurry up and hand over your valuables and be on your way."

"In my saddlebag, my wad and a gold timepiece I won me fair an' square at the poker table," McDukes said. He reached for the bag, figuring to get a grip on the six-shooter he was packing.

The trapper stopped him. "Just toss it down, cowboy, and leave the rest to me."

Heaving the bag straight at the trapper

and throwing him off-balance, McDukes leaped off the mustang and wrestled the trapper to the ground.

The trapper lost his grip on the shotgun as they rolled around in the dirt, trading kicks and punches before McDukes got a solid hold of the weapon, jumped to his feet, and turned it on the trapper, firing without hesitation.

The shot caught the trapper in the chest, killing him instantly.

To be certain, McDukes emptied the second barrel into the trapper's face.

There was no time to dig a proper grave, obliging him to deliver some final thoughts over the trapper's lifeless body. "God, that fella lying dead there meant to kill me more than I needed to kill him. You knew that before I got hold of the shotgun. Besides, my trigger finger ain't ever failed me yet. Amen."

That said, McDukes moved Rachel Stump from his mustang onto the trapper's gelding, lashed the trapper's string of four mules to the gelding, and took to the trail again, traveling at a steady pace before stopping for some much-needed sleep around a slow-burning campfire.

He made Rachel as comfortable as possible, using the trapper's saddle for a pillow and covering her with a horse blanket; then he stoked the fire and settled down for the night, easing into a sleep that didn't last long, broken by the battle cry of a half-breed charging at him with a knife meant for his heart.

McDukes rolled out of the way as the half-breed struck.

The blade dug into the dirt.

McDukes shoved the half-breed into the campfire.

The half-breed yowled, the flames scorching his bare back and buckskin pants. He leaped to his feet and jumped onto McDukes, riding him like a horse. Then he wrapped an arm around McDukes's throat, causing McDukes to pass out before he could reach the revolver he was crawling after.

The half-breed snatched up the revolver, shouted a victory cry to the star-filled sky, and took careful aim at McDukes.

Bang!

The gunshot echoed in all directions.

The half-breed studied the revolver with curiosity before he fell dead on the spot.

McDukes roused, uncertain how long he was out, startled by the sight of the half-breed asleep for keeps on a pillow of his own blood.

He recognized the voice saying, "Good thing I came along when I did, McDukes, before this half-breed, nothing more than a mere boy, took your measure and spoilt your reputation, wouldn't you say so?"

"Buchanan!"

"None but." Buchanan stepped into view on horseback, holstering his Peacemaker. "Two minutes later would have been two minutes too late."

"So I owe you again, for saving my hide one more time." McDukes picked himself up and dusted himself off. "What got you traveling these parts, Ned?"

"Come to spring you from Ford Prison and found me instead," Swaney said, riding into view. "Looks like we both was lucky to get out of that death trap when we did. Is that the nurse I see over there?"

"Also Soaring Eagle's wife," McDukes said.

Swaney said, "She was fine by me back in the hospital. Maybe best we should let her meet her god in peace and give her a proper burial."

McDukes said, "What's it about you, Swaney, that always has you saying to leave for dead the ladies in my keep, starting back with my wife, Ellie?"

Swaney tried not to show emotion. "Not

the right time or place for that conversation, McDukes. How's the nurse looking to you, Ned?"

Buchanan had been on his haunches checking her condition. He said, "She's fighting the good fight, Lowell. She might last until we reach Casa Pleach."

Swaney gave his mount a hard kick and rode on. He sensed his day of reckoning with McDukes closer at hand, maybe even lacking the circumstances he once counted on, but never seemed to find or create; that set him to wondering if McDukes felt likewise about the woman who reminded him so much of Ellie, the whore he also felt a fondness for, Jeanne d'Evreaux.

CHAPTER 16

Jeanne d'Evreaux was on her way to Tap Dance, making her own adventure without Swaney or McDukes or even Cactus Billy Clemens. The infant inside her belonged to one of them, maybe even to the one who cared about her most, but her time belonged to another who cared, Dr. Marion Wilson Beverage.

They had traded trains once already. Now, the doctor and mother-to-be were waiting for the second of three more transfers in a joyous journey that promised to bring them both a new life. Their stay in Tunneyville might be for a few weeks, maybe longer, waiting out word the threat of ongoing train robberies and Indian attacks had abated.

The trains resumed service after a week.

Despite the railroad's assurances, two days later a band of Indians followed a train's progress, according to the *Tunneyville Gazette.* Crewmen and passengers reached for brakes and bell cords to alert the engineer before unleashing fearful shouts, screams, and cries. Not many miles away from town, the Indians moved on, giving Jeanne and Dr. Beverage confidence the train they'd be boarding would also prove safe. They were correct, until a bent trestle prevented an advance on their journey.

Waiting out repairs proved hot, sticky, and dull.

Hubert Whitney, an acquaintance made when the journey left the station, suggested to the doctor he join with others passing the hours over a game of poker. Dr. Beverage gladly accepted the invitation, unaware Whitney's personal charm included his way with a deck of pasteboards. It took Beverage no time at all to lose several hundred dollars and push away from the table.

Whitney called after him: "You're more than welcome back for another tangle with the picture pasties, good doctor, if you have sufficient resources to pursue and recoup your losses."

The train was on the move again when words filtered back to Dr. Beverage that Whitney had been caught cheating all along, using a marked deck and aces up his sleeves to rake in one pot after the next. He fled the table, the other players in pursuit, and lost his footing moving from one car to the next dodging a hail of bullets except for one that caught him in the back, causing the tinhorn gambler to trip and fall off the speeding train, taking his winnings with him.

A scheduled overnight stop allowed the train to refuel, load additional freight, and, in the morning, board any additional passengers.

Dr. Beverage and Jeanne, dissatisfied with the meager accommodations offered at the train depot, checked into a hotel within walking distance. It was hardly more elegant, but at least had fresh-smelling linen on the bed and barely used towels on the bathroom rack.

As was his habit, Beverage checked Jeanne's condition and guided her into swallowing two tablespoons of tonic before they retired for the night. He was barely settled under the covers when the door crashed open and two cowpokes looking like they were fresh off a long ride stomped inside, brandishing Army-issue weapons.

"You a doctor, that so?" said the one in desperate need of a wash and shave, his voice as menacing as the hard stare in his midnight-black cat's eyes. "Let me hear your answer loud and clear, unless you're of a mind to earn a bullet between your eyes."

Dr. Beverage answered with a meek "yes."

"Not good enough. I said 'loud and clear.' "

The doctor shouted: "Yes!"

"Much better. Now get yourself dressed, the lady also. You're both coming with us."

"Just me," Dr. Beverage said.

"Who told you you could give orders?" the other cowpoke said, stroking his wild-cherry-red chin whiskers. He gun-butted the doctor at the side of the head. "There's more where that come from, you don't do what you're told, Doc."

"He will, we both will," Jeanne said, and slipped out of bed.

The cowpokes noted her condition and laughed.

The one with the midnight-black eyes said, "Our bastard luck, Kansas. Too big a belly for fancy fucking."

Dr. Beverage said, "Please, I don't mind coming with you, but you see she's expecting. Let her stay behind for safety's sake and out of kindness."

The outburst earned him another whack on the head from Kansas, who said, "We're not here for safety or for kindness. Doc. We got needs. You help, that's all. She's coming along to see you do your best. Anything less, I guarantee you, sure as hell we'll do our worst."

They had a spare horse waiting, causing the need for Dr. Beverage and Jeanne to double-up. Hard riding got them to an outlaw encampment as night was dissolving into a misty morning. The doctor refused to budge any further unless he was allowed to check Jeanne's condition. They growled, but agreed. To his satisfaction and relief, the trip had caused only minor irritation of no lasting consequence.

Among the dozen men waiting for him in the oversized, rundown log cabin were three suffering bullet wounds. The one hardest hit was their leader, whose left leg was struck beyond repair below the kneecap, exposing whole bone and bits of metal. Festering green pus told the rest of the story.

"Welcome, Dr. Bones," the leader said, practicing shameless grace. "My lousy luck and your misfortune we got thrown together like this. You keep me breathing and maybe I'll oblige likewise."

Dr. Beverage, devoid of emotion, described the depth of the leader's wound and the only solution.

The leader swallowed the ugly news like

home mash and spoke up after a few minutes of silent contemplation. "Leg or life, you say? That's a beggar's teapot for sure. Get rid of the damn thing then, and banks we visit down the trail will call me 'Gimp' for certain."

One of his men said, "You trust what you're hearing, Big Nose?"

"It is what it is, Mitch, unless you think you can do me better."

"Wish I could, Big Nose," Mitch said, his voice cracking. "I'm counting on you to pull through this, so don't go and disappoint me and the boys."

Big Nose forced a grin and gave Mitch a high sign. "Okay, Dr. Bones, I'm ready as I'll ever be."

Dr. Beverage directed preparations. The meal tables were pushed together to form an operating table and given a thorough scrubbing. Kerosene lamps were positioned to provide the best possible lighting. Whiskey was poured over all surfaces, coverings, instruments, a cleaver, and into Big Nose. The doctor wanted him passed-out drunk and feeling no pain before he began.

Meanwhile, he ministered to the two other wounded men, both of whom had been shot in the arm. In turn, he dug out the bullet and, to foil infection, poured whiskey into the gaping hole. They both screamed from beginning to end, one mad enough to go for his Colt and turn it on the doctor.

Another of the bad men used the butt end of his Springfield to knock the gun from his grip before he could squeeze the trigger. "Don't be a fool, Craig. We need him in one piece if he's going to do a good job on Big Nose."

"He better, Leroy, or there'll be hell to pay, with me the cashier."

Big Nose was in a drunken stupor by now, singing nursery rhymes off-key and inventing lyrics where memory failed him.

Dr. Beverage had him lifted from his chair and onto the operating table.

He pointed to Kansas and told him to park a bullet between Big Nose's teeth, stained ugly brown by too many years of chewing tobacco.

"Time to bite the bullet, brother," Kansas told Big Nose.

He fumbled the bullet prying open Big Nose's mouth.

Big Nose neglected to bite, and the bullet slid down his throat.

"Let me," Leroy said. "Big Nose, I'm putting a bullet between your dentals. You bite down hard to hold it in place, understand?"

Big Nose sang his answer to the tune of

"London Bridge is Falling Down."

Leroy got the bullet in place. "Good man, Big Nose. Keep pressing down now."

"I will," Big Nose said, and the bullet slid down his whiskey-lined gullet.

Dr. Beverage instructed them to substitute a length of wood for the bullet.

"I have a better idea," Craig said, and brought the handle of his Colt down on Big Nose's head. "He's out and there's more where that come from."

Satisfied, the doctor scrubbed his hands with whiskey and picked up the cleaver.

The wound was more severe than Dr. Beverage first thought.

The infection covered more ground than a scared rabbit.

The doctor bandaged what remained of the left leg and broke the news.

Craig said, "If that's so and you are a praying man, Dr. Bones, this would be a good time to begin praying for your salvation, in case Big Nose's doesn't work out too well."

Dr. Beverage pulled a well-thumbed Bible from his satchel and began reading aloud. Almost at once, gang members joined him, reciting the more familiar passages, and before the hour passed were singing Sunday school hymns of their childhood.

The doctor began to think he and Jeanne

had a good chance of surviving their ordeal.

The Lord's Prayer proved especially popular, obliging Dr. Beverage to recite it four different times, once joined by Kansas, who sang it a cappella to sustained applause and moving several of the gang to tears.

Dr. Beverage read from Romans: "Let love be genuine; hate what is evil, hold fast to what is good; love one another with brotherly affection; outdo others in showing honor." From Acts he drew: "The times of ignorance God overlooked, but now he commands all men everywhere to repent, because he has fixed a day on which he will judge the word in righteousness."

Both times he had gang members expressing their agreement and approval, peppering their reactions with shouts of "Amen" and "Hallelujah."

The next day, Dr. Beverage was reading from First Corinthians, *You cannot drink the cup of the Lord and the cup of the demons,* when Leroy signaled the news that Big Nose had breathed his last. The doctor hadn't noticed the cabin go silent and continued reading: "For the body does not consist of one member but of many. If the foot should say, 'Because I am not a hand, I do not belong to the body,' that would not make it any less a part of the body. And if the ear should say, 'Because I am not an eye, I do not belong to the body,' that would not make it any less a part of the body. If the whole body —"

Leroy cut him off. "Your patient just died, Doc. Enough with the Good Book."

Dr. Beverage set down his Bible and looked anxiously across the room at his precious Jeanne. She was teary-eyed, as were most of the gang members, and grabbed at her belly, as if she was experiencing sudden pains.

Wiping his face dry, Craig said, "Well, Dr. Bones, that sad news is not at all healthy for you, remember? You can find it in your Bible where it says 'an eye for an eye,' so there is no time like the present to abide by God Almighty's words. Grab him, boys."

Dr. Beverage submitted without a struggle.

They moved Big Nose off the surgery table, spread-eagled the doctor in his place, and used lariats to secure him.

While whiskey was being forced down his throat, Jeanne was strapped to a straight-back chair positioned to view the surgery they intended performing on Dr. Beverage.

She begged for mercy on his behalf, in return received silence and the offer of whiskey for herself, which she declined out of concern for the well-being of her unborn child.

Dr. Beverage, drunk and on the verge of passing out, called to her: "I love you with all my heart, my precious Jeanne. Try to remember. Do that for me, will you?"

"I will, good doctor, on my honor, to my dying breath and afterward," she said, and watched with increasing horror as Leroy washed the cleaver in whiskey.

Raised it high.

With one mighty thrust took the doctor's left leg above the knee.

"That scores us even," Leroy said.

Mitch took the cleaver from him and without hesitation chopped off Dr. Beverage's other leg. "That makes me feel a million times better about what you did to Big Nose," he said; then tossed the cleaver aside and left the cabin.

Inside of an hour, the gang had buried Big Nose and the doctor, packed, saddled up, and rode off.

Jeanne had screamed and passed out when Leroy dropped the cleaver on Dr. Beverage and was still unconscious when they left.

Nobody bothered to free her from her bonds.

When she began to rouse, she sensed somebody entering the cabin and a hand reaching out for her. She fought to open her eyes and discover who it was.

CHAPTER 17

Swaney and McDukes followed Ned Buchanan's lead to that great outlaw refuge, Casa Pleach, lugging along the dying Rachel Stump.

It wasn't the best place to be going.

That's known now to any connoisseur of the dime weeklies, but not then, when, the way Buchanan eventually told it, events were making history and only the retelling making heroes.

Waiting for them was Lonely Todd Logan, who had spent the time smitten with Sweet Katy Pleach, young and giddy daughter of the Casa's namesake, Dr. Ingmar Pleach.

Sweet Katy was pretty as a storybook princess. Although she had developed a similar affection for Logan, she preferred variety. She surrendered all her luxuries to him except true love, explaining frequently she relished herself as a student of lust.

"It's more fun and educational with

strangers," she said. "Each one brings me a different mystery that I take pleasure in unlocking."

"Which mystery am I?" Logan wondered early in their relationship.

Sweet Katy giggled and illustrated her answer without spoken comment.

After Buchanan told him his plan to spring McDukes from prison and asked Logan to wait for him at Casa Pleach, Logan crawled into bed with Sweet Katy and raised the question like he was asking it for the first time.

She giggled. "Mine to know and yours to find out, silly."

"Tell me something, anything, won't you, please? Loving you's hard enough when I got no true love coming back, Sweet Katy."

"You're better," she said. "That's something."

"I need more'n that." He ran through names, mostly desperadoes who came and went after short stays, and heard, "Not the lover I got in mind, silly."

Out of frustration, he said, "Better'n Ned Buchanan?"

"No, you silly boy."

"How about your father?" Logan said.

"Poppa Ingmar doesn't do it much since my sister's gone. He always thought it made more sense the three of us sharing family pleasures. I don't know if I agree, but fathers know best, it's said."

"Now who's the silly one, Sweet Katy? That's some sense of humor you're packing."

She dropped her grin. "He'd kill you, you know, he ever found out I told you, so keep it our little secret, promise?"

"Wouldn't he also kill you?"

"Of course not, you silly boy. I'm his daughter. Poppa Ingmar loves me."

Had she made up the story? Logan couldn't be sure, but didn't want to think otherwise.

"Whatever you say, Sweet Katy."

"I knew I could trust you," she said, smothering him in kisses. "You are too marvelous for words, Lonely Todd Logan. You'll never be lonely when I'm around. Never, never, never."

She was on him again like white on rice, and thereafter always had fanciful stories to go with their lovemaking

Poppa Ingmar, she said, came to America from the Old Country stowed away on a tramp steamer. He was tall, blond, and handsome, built like an unfinished meal, and had a cheeky smile and way with women that he always used for personal gain.

He worked the railroads before he hired on as an undertaker's assistant and made a habit of inheriting property the newly deceased no longer had need for. He came to own a worn doctor's satchel, announced himself a doctor, and traveled the country for years, hawking colored sugar and honey water as a cure-all for every disease known to mankind, called Dr. Pleach's Miracle Tonic and Body Rub.

He settled for a time in Mother Lode but moved on to escape the Injun challenges to life and limb, wealthy enough by now to acquire remote acreage sufficient to create Casa Pleach as a secret haven exclusively for desperadoes dodging the long reach of law and order. It caught on at once and made Poppa Ingmar even richer, especially after he recognized there was greater profit in burying the dead than in saving the living, and reinvented himself as an undertaker.

"What about your mother?" Logan thought to ask one time.

"We don't talk about her," Sweet Katy said. "She's dead. One day she wasn't and then she was."

"Your sister?"

"Her either."

"Also dead?"

"No, you silly boy. Poppa was so jealous after Lucy got swept off her feet with promises of eternal love and left for keeps with the Colorado Kid that he disowned her name and memory and banished her forever from his say and sight."

"That was her name — Lucy?"

"Could be. I think so. I'm not sure anymore."

On the trail to Casa Pleach, Swaney and McDukes sat around the campfire one quiet night over smokes and coffee, sharing stories about their good times together before life turned darker than ever and ruptured their friendship.

The Quirt business, of course, the true story, not the version built way out of proportion by Frank Leslie and the other dime weekly writers who never let truth interfere with the larger-than-life fantasies they spun.

The one about the Lancaster gold mine got good laughs, especially the part where Bear Stands Tall was on the verge of making a meal of McDukes until Swaney thought to trade him for the fresh carcass of Blackjack Walters, who had just proven slower on the draw than Swaney.

On and on, the laughs growing louder and warmer until Swaney said, "Are you still bent on killing me, McDukes?"

McDukes's expression turned sour. "Yep."

"It wasn't the way you think it was, McDukes."

"Eyes ain't lies, Swaney."

"The military made it sound different from what it actually was, McDukes."

McDukes answered him with a blank look, rose, crushed his smoke under his boot, and left the comfort of the campfire.

Swaney, with Ned Buchanan for company, said, "You know the truth, Ned?"

Buchanan had no answer for him.

They both looked after McDukes, neither doubting his mind had turned to memories of Ellie, the woman he made his wife.

Ellie had that look peculiar to French women, her father, Bellesiles by name, being from that neck of the world. He was a sodbuster, his few acres good for wheat and little else, except, maybe, for some cattle and sheep to supplement the family income.

Came a time, railroad people had need for the land.

They offered Bellesiles a fair price, but he had no interest in selling and politely turned them away. Undeterred, they came back several times afterward, always with an increased offer. Bellesiles stood firm. The railroad people, equally resolute, took drastic action.

Two gunslingers rode up to the farm the day of the tragedy, Wretched Daniel Davidson and Soo Fong Yo Han, killers on the railroad payroll, hired to keep the workers in line and to fix other problems brought to their attention.

Wretched Daniel was carrying three Colts, two holstered and the other stuck inside his boot. Soo Fong Yo Han was packing a custom long-barrel and a Winchester short rifle, as well as a shotgun loaded with pistol balls.

Bellesiles strolled out of the tall grass. He carried either a hoe or a rake, depending on which dime weekly account you read. He wiped the sweat off his brow with an over-sized handkerchief, and gave them a polite smile.

Wretched Daniel said, "We're bringin' you a fair and final offer from our employers, old man. In my saddlebag is more'n a thousand dollars. That sum will buy you better land elsewhere down the rail line, so take it and save your loved ones any cause for regret."

"Tell them I told you to say changing the

route would be easier than trying to have me change my mind," Bellesiles said as he turned and headed for the tall grass.

Wretched Daniel called out, "He threatened me!"

"I see it good," Soo Fong Yo Han said.

Between them they emptied a pound of hot lead into Bellesiles.

He fell dead on the spot.

Wretched Daniel kicked Bellesiles's lifeless body over onto his back and with Soo Fong Yo Han added eight bullets to his chest and stomach. He fired two shots into the air before he turned the Peacemaker on Soo Fong Yo Han, shot him in the shoulder, and placed the gun in Bellesiles's hand, finger on the trigger.

"I keepin' count," Soo Fong Yo Han said, putting pressure on his wound. "Next time you take bullet."

"What's fair is fair, Soo. Anyhow, you seen him threaten me an' shoot first."

"I did, and you see him shoot me. Any jury call it self-defense, like other times before."

"I saw enough to know it was murder," McDukes said, stepping out of the tall grass.

He had been enjoying the family's hospitality at the time, a hot meal and a comfortable bed overnight in the spirit of friendship common to the open plains. He should have left already, but was transfixed by the Gallic beauty of the Frenchman's daughter, Ellie, inventing excuses to linger a while longer.

The sound of the shots alarmed Ellie. "Father never carries a weapon," she said. "He does not believe in violence."

McDukes told her to stay put, grabbed his six-shooter, and raced off.

"Your word agin ours, cowboy," Wretched Daniel said, forcing a laugh.

"Him and me," Soo Fong Yo Han said, joining the laughter. "Self-defense."

"If that's how you care to play it, maybe we best settle the score here and now."

"You threatenin' us, cowboy?" Wretched Daniel said, and went after one of his holstered Colts.

McDukes was faster. He put a bullet into Wretched Daniel with squint-eyed accuracy.

Eyeing Soo Fong Yo Han, McDukes said, "You next, Chinaman."

Soo Fong Yo Han stained his pants and dropped his weapons, fell to his knees, hands clenched, begging McDukes for mercy.

"Like you showed poor Mr. Bellesiles? I hardly think so."

At that moment, Ellie Bellesiles came running through the grass into the space between McDukes and Soo Fong Yo Han, urging McDukes not to fire. "My father will tell you there has been enough killing already," she said.

The distraction gave Soo Fong Yo Han time to grab his rifle and jump up, take hold of Ellie, and jam the Winchester into her trim waist. "You go, let me ride away or she dead girl for certain," he said.

McDukes had been in similar showdowns before. There was no doubt in his mind he could take the Chinaman, but this was no ordinary standoff. He didn't want to gamble with Ellie's life or ignore her wishes. From the moment she welcomed him into the cabin and smiled at him for the first time, he understood this beautiful creature was meant to be his mate. Her smile was enough to bring tears of joy to his eyes.

Soo Fong Yo Han said, "I count three. You still here, her life ends."

Ellie said, "Please, Mr. McDukes. I pray you do as he says. I will be fine. The Lord will protect me."

"One."

"Mr. McDukes, let him go his own way. Please. For my dear father, if not for me."

"Two."

McDukes said, "Best I protect you, in case the Lord's busy elsewhere," and fired.

His shot zipped past Ellie and caught Soo Fong Yo Han in his right kneecap.

Soo Fong Yo Han tilted off-balance, lost his grip on her, dropped the Winchester, and fell to the ground clutching his wounded knee, screaming in pain and at McDukes in his native tongue.

Ellie stepped away from him and started for McDukes, but suddenly froze, stunned by the sight of her father's bloody, bullet-mutilated body. Her look of relief and gratitude melted away. She stepped back to Soo Fong Yo Han and stooped to retrieve his Winchester. "Did you see? He killed my father," she said; then aimed, blew Soo Fong Yo Han's head from his neck, threw the rifle into the tall grass, and headed back to the cabin.

McDukes helped Ellie pack after the bodies were buried, only her father's grave marked by a cross and prayed over. He urged her to take only necessities. Anything else could be bought with the greenbacks he found in Wretched Daniel's saddlebag, a thousand in total, making them rich by common standards.

She was most concerned about a small daguerreotype of her father and long-dead mother; a photograph made on a piece of copper covered in silver, mounted in a plain silver crutch frame. *"Mon père, ma mère,"* she said solemnly, but without tears.

Three days and nights on the trail, McDukes and Ellie had shared enough confidences to care about sharing more.

She said, "Even though I'm now a killer?"

"An avenging angel, more like it."

"And you, Mr. McDukes?"

"Most of the time only a killer."

"Then I'm obliged to come along for keeps and sometimes lend you my halo," she said, touching his arm with all the tenderness of a kiss.

Shortly, they came across an itinerant preacher and paid him a handsome price to conduct the ceremony, making their union official.

"You, Mrs. McDukes, are quite the most beautiful woman I ever made a wife," the preacher said, laying a discreet kiss on the bride's cheek. "Mr. McDukes, watch over her with loving care. She is the kind can get juices flowing whenever menfolk come around."

"More than juices, blood will flow I see anyone, even a friend, casting a hungry eye in the direction of Mrs. McDukes, sir."

And now, having suffered enough palaver about Ellie with Swaney and Buchanan,

McDukes returned to the campfire and picked a new subject for conversation.

He traveled farther back in the past, to a time before he first saw Ellie, his first full year of riding with another established hero of the dime weeklies, Lowell Swaney. It was at a time Wyatt Earp busied himself being a lawman when he wasn't operating a gambling parlor with his brothers, enjoying curious friendships with that bad cavity of a dentist, Holliday, and consorting with Masterson, the city slicker who brandished a fancy Buntline to chop down people like so much tall timber.

Swaney tossed some branches on the campfire and helped himself to a fresh mug of java.

"I respect Earp, but that corral showdown was his doing and not played fair and square, no matter who I asked or how," Swaney said.

Buchanan said, "You ever get a word of defense out of Wyatt?"

"He laughed in my face, twirled his rod, claimed to be faster than me, and invited me to try him outside if I doubted his boast."

"What did you do about it?" McDukes said.

"Nothing. I may be crazy, but I ain't stupid."

McDukes said, "Wyatt and me, we had words over the poker table, me wondering if all his decks come with five aces, one for up his sleeve. Wyatt gives me a hard look, like he's filling in for the Grim Reaper, and says, 'You accusing me of cheating, McDukes?' He's got a gun sitting by his chips an' Holliday, who's in the game, pulls out a Derringer and slaps it down on the table. Corner of my eye, I see one of the Earp brothers by the bar. He's also packing."

"How did you talk your way out of that damn spot?"

"I didn't. I drew my Colts and got myself killed three ways from Sunday."

Swaney was unable to sleep their last night out before reaching Casa Pleach.

He thought about the good times and the bad with McDukes.

It was one for one and one for the other in equal measure back then. All they owed each other by now was each other, yet here was McDukes — who should know better — still blaming him and promising revenge for the death of his woman, although he knew Swaney had loved and respected Ellie as much as he did.

McDukes was as crazy now as then, when the colonel broke the news to him and placed the mantle of blame squarely upon Swaney, explaining, "He was jealous of your love and for that reason did his foul deed."

McDukes broke down over the news, but, worse yet, he believed the part about Swaney. He told as much to Buchanan, who arrived too late to prevent the damage, but managed to delay the showdown McDukes swore was coming.

Buchanan said, "You rage in the wrong direction, McDukes. Kill the men who made her the way Ellie became, not him."

"I been told better, Ned. It happened as if Swaney pulled the trigger himself. My Ellie were alive until he put that rod to her temple."

"Was other rods killed your woman, not his."

McDukes seemed on the verge of drawing against Buchanan for telling him what he had no intention of believing. Only Buchanan's firm stand prevented that miscarriage.

"McDukes, you have turned madder than a loon," Buchanan said. "You believe that bastard of a colonel, who you had loathing for before this, over Swaney. Shame on you for taking on as the truth his mealy-mouthed words that put Swaney in the worst possible repute."

Buchanan's words meant nothing to McDukes.

McDukes's mind was made up.

Swaney was guilty.

Swaney would pay the price.

"I mean to have him my way, under my terms of vengeance and relief," McDukes said, "make him suffer, same as me, by taking from him all that matters most."

He made his move after Swaney had served four years of a seven-year sentence at Desert Prison, caused by the colonel's cunning. McDukes tracked down Buchanan and said, "Ned, I need your special skills to bring me and Swaney together."

"I'd hoped by now you'd quit on your crazy thoughts about revenge, McDukes."

"Crazy like a prairie chicken. I still mean to have Swaney under my terms, in an urgent, violent, raging fashion exceeding the shame he set upon my house."

"McDukes, no good can ever come of that. Abandon that kind of folly."

"Stop your song, Ned. How do we break him out of Desert Prison?"

Buchanan surrendered to folly. "First I need you to be inside," he said.

■ ■ ■

McDukes also was having a bad night, also about Ellie, going farther back than anything Swaney said or Buchanan may have been thinking, almost to the beginning; what he knew and what he learned.

He was off hunting game for food with Ruben Garner, a queer cuss who had attached himself to the couple. She usually joined him, but today the mother-to-be was feeling the flush of sickness and stomach gyrations that often signal impending birth.

Swaney, the heroic, white-frocked plainsman of the dime weeklies, scouting for the military at the time, was there visiting. He insisted on staying longer than planned, to look after Ellie until McDukes returned.

That evening, Ellie set off by herself on a short stroll through the township gardens. She said she needed some time to herself, half an hour at most. Swaney bent to her wish, a choice he would soon come to regret.

The sky was pitch black, the moon invisible, no stars to light her walk, when Ellie was grabbed, dragged behind a tall row of hedges, and raped. She fainted, stirred awake only to realize she was being raped again. She lost count of how many times and how many ways by how many men, all taking great pleasure in brutalizing her.

After an hour passed and Ellie had not returned, Swaney went looking for her.

She was barely recognizable when he found her, the damage to her face severe, her half-naked body evidence of the beatings she had endured, further reason to believe she had lost the baby. She struggled to tell him all she knew for certain was that they wore military uniforms.

Swaney covered her up, ministered as best he could to her condition, and took her to the military encampment, where an investigation was immediately organized by a sympathetic commander, Colonel Francis Milstead Keepers.

"I know the men who signed out, but mind you, Swaney, and you, dear Mrs. McDukes, I have difficulty believing any soldier serving under me could be capable of so dreadful, wrong, and spiteful an act of aggression upon fair womanhood."

A squad of blue britches was summoned to the colonel's office and lined up.

Ellie, somehow mustering the strength to walk, moved from one soldier to the next, staring each in the face, but ultimately was unable to fix blame on any of them.

Swaney demanded another squad be summoned for inspection.

Colonel Keepers had carefully kept away
every soldier who signed out, but he obliged
Swaney before the scout's temper grew
louder and exploded into violence, as it
often did in the dime weekly tales of his
adventures.

At that moment, Ellie McDukes swooned.

Swaney grabbed for her and missed.

She fell to the floor, a bag of screams.

Sitting up, thinking she was still on her
devastating walk, she begged for mercy,
spread her legs, and used her fingers to
reproduce some of the indignities heaped
upon her.

Swaney attempted to help her up.

She pushed him away, snatched the pistol
laying within reach on the colonel's desk,
and scrambled to a far corner of the room,
where she waved the weapon threateningly
while tearing at her clothing, too fast for
anyone to prevent her self-inflicted shame.

The colonel's young orderly started for
her, offering his jacket as cover.

"Enough," Ellie, indifferent to her naked-
ness, screamed at him: "Not one more step."

"I mean you no harm, missus," he said, in
a voice meant to calm her.

"No harm? My baby is dead before taking

246

a first breath, so what harm is left for you or anybody to do me?"

She fired.

The orderly caught the bullet in his chest and, mortally wounded, studied her in bloody disbelief before dropping onto the floor facedown.

Swaney said, "Enough, dear lady. I beg you to put down the gun before more damage is done. I swear to you we'll identify the true villains and see that justice is served."

She answered by choosing a soldier at random and killing him.

After him, a third soldier.

"There is how justice is best served," Ellie said.

She appeared to smile with satisfaction and lowered the pistol, but only for seconds before she jammed the barrel into her mouth and squeezed the trigger.

When he arrived to claim Ellie's body, McDukes went berserk at the sight of her.

He charged at Colonel Francis Milstead Keepers. "You and your blue britches are the cause of my wife's death," he shouted. "I mean to have my revenge."

He was forcibly restrained by the colonel's men.

The colonel said, "Who told you that,

McDukes?"

"Lowell Swaney, the first to find Ellie and hear her story."

"Of course, it was, Swaney looking after his own backside by feeding you that canard. Settle down and hear the truth from me, so help me God." He raised his right hand like he was swearing an oath.

"Settled enough. Let's hear it."

"It was Swaney himself who attacked, beat, and raped your wife, McDukes. She named him to me in front of witnesses, in front of Swaney himself, before taking her own sweet life, unable to shed the guilt she felt over losing the child inside her."

"Swaney?"

"Him who was supposed to look after her, protect her from harm, while you were off hunting with your friend here, Ruben Garner."

"Swaney?" McDukes said, barely able to scrounge out the name a second time.

Colonel Keepers said, "She pointed a finger at him, called his name, and — you already know the rest."

"Swaney," McDukes said. "You hear that, Rube?"

"Heard fine, McDukes. Now it's time to take Ellie back home with us."

"Don't you worry none," the colonel assured McDukes. "We have Swaney in custody. Justice will prevail."

"My kind of justice, if not yours, Colonel Keepers."

The known facts, such as they were, gave rise to stories in the dime weeklies and even the possibly more reliable publications like *Harper's Weekly, The Illustrated London News,* even *Godey's Lady's Book,* and, to be sure, *The National Police Gazette.*

They told of a "Scarlet Avenger," true identity unknown, who targeted blue britches for death, to the exclusion of others.

McDukes was the likely villain, given his passion for revenge, but there was nothing to confirm his guilt or explain why it was the military he was making war against.

Traps were set for him, delicious bait made available, but he always eluded capture by the soldiers, who almost came close the night his target was an ambitious, career-driven lieutenant who enjoyed the patronage of Colonel Francis Milstead Keepers.

The lieutenant played obnoxious drunk at the town bars this particular attempt — or so it was reported in the pages of *Frank Leslie's Weekly,* by Leslie himself, who wrote it as an eyewitness account. At a prescribed hour, the lieutenant bid a loud, loathsome farewell to everyone and set off by himself on the empty streets.

For effect, he took nips from an uncapped bottle of sour mash as he clunked along the slat-board sidewalk before sloshing across the muddy road and wandering into a side alley, singing "Fair Lady of the Easy Virtue," the version that bordered on bawdy, giving it the special cavalry emphasis that made the fairest maidens blush.

"Fair lady of the easy virtue," he sang. "Nothing to sneeze at though I go kerchoo."

He stopped, thinking he heard boots tracking him; then he leaned against a sidewall and took a swig of mash before starting in again, off-key, "Fair lady of the easy virtue, nothing to sneeze at though I go kerchoo. Where I was dry, I got me wet. Where I am hot, I'll get you yet. Kerchoo. Kerchoo. Kerchoo."

That was the last verse the lieutenant sang before two shots rang out and connected with his belly. He crashed backward into the wall before stumbling forward and falling facedown into a rain puddle.

Only heavy cushions of metal-lined leather stuffed inside his uniform saved the lieutenant from death.

He pushed onto his feet and was grabbed from behind by someone thought to be the Scarlet Avenger, who clutched a ten-inch Bowie he intended to use on either the lieutenant's throat or scalp.

A shot from a .50 caliber Sharps knocked the knife from his grip, the work of one of a dozen sharpshooters ordered to protect the lieutenant and now pouring out of their hiding places.

Somehow, the Scarlet Avenger managed to use the darkness to lose himself among the soldiers and disappear. A thorough canvas of the streets and structures turned up no one, adding to the legend fabricated by all the publications in the interest of raising circulation and profits.

Much of the truth would emerge later, provided by Ruben Garner.

CHAPTER 18

Ruben Garner and Little Tad Logan grew to know each other well while riding the trails together in the days after their retreat from Atonement and a parting of the ways from McDukes, whose damaged memory had him believing he was Lowell Swaney.

Garner told Logan what he knew of the deception, also what he knew of the real Lowell Swaney, but not everything. Only after a while did he get around to the tale of the wrangle that put Swaney in prison and, in the bargain, put Garner into the dime weeklies.

"When the bother began, Oscar Prettyman and me were wrangling a herd of ailing horses about two hundred miles due north of central," Garner said, chewing every word with the same caution he used cutting strays from the herd.

Most of the horses had feasted on locoweed. Those not yet dead were on the ground and into fits, some groaning, others groaning and foaming at the mouth. Another bunch had caught the Plains disease that turned them hairless and shivering, nostrils swollen and running, eyes like gushers, struggling to breathe; open kidney sores adding to the ugly sight.

The dozen healthy horses left had been moved to a safe location. How long they would last was a giant question fit for a heifer in heat.

Prettyman said, "I can't take any more of this, partner. What say we take off with them and the chuck wagon?"

"Relief is heading our way, Oscar. Another day or two is all we're looking at."

Prettyman wasn't satisfied with Garner's answer.

They argued for hours and were still at it over a dinner of bacon and beans.

Somewhere into his second cup of java, Garner swooned. Prettyman had salted Garner's pour with locoweed grounds. Garner started foaming at the mouth, his bloodshot eyes blazing like Fourth of July pinwheels. Every joint ached, every muscle burned.

Prettyman rode off with the healthy horses roped to the back of the chuck wagon, leaving Garner to die.

"I come out of it alive and to this day can't figure how that happened, but thankful for the outcome," Garner told Logan. "I set my mind on one piece of business. It took me better than a year, but I managed to track down that pus ball, Oscar Prettyman."

He found him in the town of Buffalo Chips.

Prettyman had done well for himself, trading the horses and the wagon for ownership of a profitable general store, whose proprietor was hungry to test his luck in the exploding gold fields of California.

Garner woke Prettyman from a deep sleep by poking a Peacemaker into his cheek and ordering him out of bed and into his britches. He roped Prettyman's hands behind his back and led him through empty side streets at gunpoint to the town's buffalo pens, where he forced him onto his knees and roped his ankles together.

All the while Prettyman tried talking himself back into Garner's good graces. Garner ignored him, reserving his only reply for the moment before he turned to walk away, a simple, "Adios, Oscar." Garner then approached the buffaloes cautiously, prodding one after another in a manner that led to snorting and pawing and inspired a rampage that caught Prettyman under their hooves.

Garner waited for the buffaloes to settle before he checked to make sure there was no life left in Prettyman's mangled body, retrieved the telltale ropes, and headed for a peaceful night's sleep in his room at the Buffalo Chips Boarding House & Bath.

Prettyman's body was discovered in the morning.

The circumstance led the townsfolk to two theories — he was drunk and stumbled to his death or, suffering some inner demon, he decided to commit suicide and made the buffaloes his weapon of choice. One theory being as good as the other, they left it there.

Little Tad Logan said, "I don't understand then what got your play in his death known and you thrown into prison."

"Not my getting even with that rattle-snake," Garner said. "It was my old boss, whose horses Prettyman took off with. He figured the two of us were in cahoots, and nothing I said convinced him otherwise, so I got tried and sentenced for Prettyman's crime, not my own."

"Damned unfair, you ask me."

"Damned lucky, too, Logan. Instead of being found out and strung up for murder, I got sentenced to twelve years for a different crime that called for a hanging, but the circuit judge ruled leniency was in order, seeing as how taking the twelve horses saved them from dying of locoweed."

"What came of that stretch in prison? You didn't do no twelve years."

"Thanks due a cowpoke named Buchanan, sent to get me out by an old *compadre* named McDukes. That should tell you something where I might not tell you anything. I was gone from there before too many days turned into nights."

"So that's how come you figure you owe McDukes?"

"One reason in many. There are some that matter more," Garner said, soft as a coo bird, and launched a story about the time he and McDukes were holding off Indian plunderers in the dead of winter, a hole in the hillside their only protection against a killing snow that fell without letup.

Garner was wounded, knocking on death's door. McDukes was fighting off the Indians like they were targets in a carnival midway shooting gallery and threatening to kill Garner, were he crass enough to die on him.

One day rolled into the next.

Their food supply ran out.

McDukes sneaked after one of the dead Indians and dragged him into the cave, meaning for them to feed off his corpse.

Garner said he'd rather die first.

McDukes said, "You will if you don't eat."

They dined on the Indian and, when there was nothing edible left of him, they satisfied their hunger on the wasted carcass of a dead Indian pony; and after that, with regret, on their own horses.

Water fit to drink became a problem after the snow and the rain quit, causing Garner and McDukes to invoke a solution they had learned in more peaceful times from Soaring Eagle. They cut a small opening in their veins and sucked at the blood, never taking too much, only enough to moisten their swollen lips.

The Indians massed for a final assault on the cave dwellers, now too weak to successfully hold them off.

Garner and McDukes steeled themselves for a charge that never came. The Indians had fled, alarmed by the sound of a bugle signaling a cavalry troop advancing on them.

Little Tad Logan said, "How did the troop know where to find you?"

"We never asked, just glad that they did," Garner said.

"Cards on the table, Rube. Sounds to me like I been hearing some truth out of you, but more of a story invented by the dime weeklies."

Garner shrugged off the challenge. "Then take what you want as the truth and leave the rest for someone else," he said. He booted his mustang and, laughing, galloped off.

A half day down the trail, Garner got to talking again, spinning stories like a burst dam.

When he brought up Ellie McDukes's death and assigned the responsibility to Colonel Francis Milstead Keepers, Logan said, "The way I read about it for a fact, it was the doing of a certain military scout named Swaney."

"Does a gold mine always yield gold?" Garner said.

"Not always. Only a fool's paradise sometimes."

"Same with the truth, Logan. Facts and truth are not always one and the same. Facts are what we believe. Truths are what we know."

"You only confuse me, Ned."

"Same way the dime weeklies led people to confuse who caused the death of McDukes's missus."

"Your fact?"

"My truth. I come to hear it from more

than one person who knew better than McDukes. The parties responsible were Colonel Keepers and certain of the blue britches he protected from discovery at the expense of Lowell Swaney's freedom."

"What other truths do you have to share, if any?"

"Many, but one for your ears only and definitely not for sharing —"

"My word on that, Ned."

"You know of the Scarlet Avenger?"

"What I read in the dime weeklies."

"How they agreed he would one day be exposed as Ellie McDukes's grieving husband?"

"None more obvious than McDukes."

"I know better, Logan. The Scarlet Avenger is me. I am the Scarlet Avenger."

Garner waited until he and Little Tad Logan were parked for the night to share what he knew with Logan, starting from the day he and McDukes went hunting, leaving behind a pregnant Ellie in the watchful care of Swaney.

"Out for a walk by herself, blue britches snatched her and cut her down like new mown hay, ravaged and brutalized her for fun and sport, with Colonel Keepers leading the charge," Garner said. "He shifted the blame onto Swaney for obvious reasons."

"You speak those words with great authority, Rube, but I hear no proof."

"My feeling exactly as they carted Swaney off, so I set about looking for it as the Scarlet Avenger. I went after Keepers's men one after the next and got the truth out of them, got them to name names, before I sent them off to meet their Maker."

"You killed innocent men as well as the guilty ones?"

"I did, yes, in order to protect my true identity while mining truths that would show Swaney to be the innocent man I believed him to be. His friendship with McDukes and his affection for Ellie were too sincere for him to ever turn on them in so shameful a manner."

"So that's how you come to side with McDukes when he took on Keepers and the others in that saloon shootout."

"And left Keepers breathing in his bed later on, when I saw the wife by his side was the woman who endured that attack alongside us."

"The minute you knew, why didn't you let McDukes in on the truth, say, 'Keepers, not Swaney, should be the object of your revenge'?"

"Think back. When I called him by his rightful name, McDukes corrected me, saying he was Swaney, not McDukes. I didn't understand why he was being so crazy, but held my tongue, choosing to wait for his sanity to return."

"What's in store for us now, Rube, for you and me?"

"I am hot to pay Keepers's wife a return visit, feeling we share an affinity for each other."

"With me along for watching? No, sir. I'm no Peeping Tad."

"Never my intention, Logan. Choose your own recreation and we'll catch up later."

Garner waited patiently for Keepers to leave before stealing into his home through a bedroom window.

His wife, not yet asleep, wasn't alarmed to discover him.

She smiled seductively and said, "I was hoping to see you again."

Garner said, "I'm back with something special in mind."

"I was also hoping for that," she said, and threw aside the covers.

"You're naked."

"Because of the weather. Your presence makes it even hotter."

261

She worked her body to prevent any misunderstanding.

"Your husband?"

"You now, him later. The brute is off playing five card stud and won't return for hours."

"What if he does?"

"Shoot him for the dog he is, like you should have done your last visit. You planning to waste any more time talking about him, mister, or are you all talk and no action?"

Garner dropped his britches and joined her.

She proved wilder than the thoughts he'd been harboring about her, taking him far beyond the point of exhaustion.

Just him.

She was insatiable.

Before Garner left, he gave Colonel Keepers's wife a final embrace and a lingering kiss that almost set him off again.

"You will return?" she said, her throat hoarse from use.

"If that's what you want."

"You know what I want. I'm happier seeing you coming than going."

Reduced to tears, she watched him climb out the window.

Neither knew until later how soon Garner

would return to involve her in a plot to make Keepers answer for the death of Little Tad Logan.

would return to involve her in a plot to make Keepers answer for the death of Little Tad Logan.

CHAPTER 19

Little Tad Logan was overpowered leaving the gaming parlor, where the cards he drew were almost as bad as the liquor he drank.

They conked him on the head and tossed his unconscious body over a horse.

He woke roped to an upright chair in a room somewhere, under study by Colonel Francis Milstead Keepers, inhaling smoke from one of the colonel's lean cigars and the smell from the sweaty armpits and crusted clothing of his henchmen, Juan Forminfante and Pronto Leaukomia, who appeared anxious to kill him and made no secret of it.

Keepers kept them at bay.

It was news of Swaney and McDukes he was after, more than getting even with Logan for going against him in the saloon shootout. He wanted to hear what Logan knew about the so-called Scarlet Avenger who murdered so many of his men before he retired from the military.

Logan insisted he had nothing to contribute.

"You're certain, little man?"

"Yes, sir, Colonel. I'm riding alongside Ruben Garner these days and happier for it, still not knowing why McDukes was going back then by the false name Swaney, or was he Swaney passing as McDukes? It's so far back, I can't never be sure anymore."

"Why don't I believe you, little man?"

"Nobody believed Columbus when he went around saying the world was round."

"Hogwash."

"You saying the world is flat, Colonel? I'll take your word for it, sure as my name is Tad Logan."

Keepers allowed his quiet rage to simmer before he signaled Forminfante and Leaukomia with a nod and left the room.

Forminfante said, "You first, partner."

"Go ahead," Leaukomia said. "I think I went first last time."

"Not my memory, but I will," Forminfante said, and promptly stubbed out the burning butt of a hand-rolled smoke on Logan's cheek.

Logan screamed, but once again denied any knowledge of Swaney and McDukes. "Do your worst and that will still be my

265

answer," he said.

"We'll do our best, and maybe that will help you change your mind," Forminfante said.

He soaked a fist in brine before smashing Logan's face, crunching bone on one cheek, then the other, breaking Logan's jaw. He showed Logan a leather-handled butcher knife and described its intended use. The horror of his words caused Logan to faint. Two buckets of ice water woke him.

Forminfante moved the blade to Logan's neck.

"No you don't," Leaukomia said. "It's my turn. You went first, but that doesn't mean you get to have all the fun."

"You are right, partner. I apologize," Forminfante said. He handed over the knife.

Leaukomia said, "I got a better idea than slicing your throat, Logan. I'm taking your scalp with you alive to watch."

He grabbed a crop of Logan's hair.

The knife cut like a knight's ritual sword, freeing the hair from Logan's head.

Leaukomia moved nose-close to Logan, breathing stink into his bleeding eyes. "Your scalp goes next, you don't tell us right now what the colonel wants to hear," he said.

Logan was beyond speech. He managed small, barely audible, wholly involuntary little grunts of pain, nothing more.

Forminfante said, "Save the scalp for later, partner. Don't be in such a hurry-up to add a pelt to your belt. Let's play the way the Paiutes play; what do you say?"

"Why not, unless Logan got some objection. You got some objection, Logan?" Logan made an unintelligible noise. "Logan got no objection."

Together, Forminfante and Leaukomia stripped Logan of his britches and cut away the bottom of his long johns to make his private parts less private.

"It looks to be another leg," Forminfante said. "Lucky ladies for sure, them what fall into company with this man here."

Leaukomia laughed along with him and turned back to Logan.

"You got another minute, maybe two, to 'fess up, or I scalp clean your pisser real good in practice for your scalp," he said, grabbing Logan's pisser.

Logan sprang a surprise on him.

Forminfante laughed harder than ever.

Leaukomia, past the joking stage, spit a mouthful of piss at Logan. He used a shirtsleeve to wipe and dry his face, unbuttoned his fly, and answered Logan in kind. "Your time, it has run out. I do not plan to waste any more patience on you," he said.

He kicked Logan, connecting the spur on his boot with Logan's midsection. Where working cowpokes filed down spur edges to protect a pony's flanks, Leaukomia's were filed to a sharp point. He withdrew the spur after a second swift kick and brought his boot back down to the floor, the jinglebobs and heel chain making joyful music. Logan, gushing blood, passed out after managing a scream and struggling to say what sounded like, "World round."

Ruben Garner went looking for Logan after leaving the colonel's wife and couldn't find him anywhere until a tipsy saloon patron overheard him questioning the barkeep and said, "You mean Little Tad? They found him the closest thing to a corpse in some alleyway and rushed him over to old Doc Whittemore's place."

Logan was there, stretched out on the doctor's operating table, struggling to stay alive.

He managed a smile when he saw it was Garner.

"They got me good finally, and I was too weak to resist anymore," he said, struggling to be understood. "Forgive me, Rube. I spilled everything I knew."

Without prompting, he explained what

that meant.

Garner waved Logan's words away. "I owe those bastards for you now, for certain, same as Swaney and McDukes owe that damn colonel," he said.

"Hey, Rube." Garner moved an ear close to Logan's lips. "Am I going to die, Rube?"

Garner glanced over to Doc Whittemore, who nodded affirmatively.

Logan said, "Heaven and a harp in my future, Rube?"

Garner couldn't bring himself to lie. "St. Peter's anxious to meet you, Tad."

Those were the last words Logan heard.

Garner seemed mesmerized by the physical damage imposed on Little Tad, almost to the point of vomiting. "Point me at who did this to my friend and I'll show one and all the true form of justice," he murmured. "Forminfante. Leaukomia. Those are names I'll remember not to forget."

He had Doc Whittemore wrap the body and took Logan miles away, to a quiet garden of desert wildflowers he found off the well-traveled rutted wagon trails. He buried Logan and marked the grave with a simple cross. The prayer he voiced to the sky and a congregation of none was brief: "Lord, Little Tad Logan was not the best of men, but, hell, who is?"

That said, Garner headed off for a new destination, Casa Pleach, feeling ashamed that his thoughts kept shifting between Logan and Colonel Keepers's wife. If he'd stuck with Logan instead of frolicking with her, would Logan still be alive?

He wondered if McDukes had similar thoughts about Ellie.

He wondered if the colonel's wife was thinking about him.

He wondered if she —

Jesus!

She was only a "she" to him!

He had never bothered to learn her name.

Colonel Keepers's wife was still luxuriating in thoughts about Garner when her husband returned home, earlier than she figured. She was still naked, not ready yet to bathe and lose the heady perfume of their intense lovemaking. The colonel surely would recognize that scent as evidence of her unfaithfulness. With cold, self-saving calculation, she manufactured tears and flew her quaking body into his arms, babbling like a madwoman: "He took me for his own and raped me, darling. I tried to fight him off, but he was too big and strong and he raped me again and again."

"Tell me who did this to you," the colonel said, holding her tight and stroking her hair. "Give me a name, you poor thing you."

"I don't know his name."

"Can you tell me what he looked like?"

She struggled her way through a description of Garner.

"Garner, that's who I'm hearing from you. Ruben Garner. Tell me exactly what went on with him, what he did to you, so there's no question a jury will have him hanging from a tree the minute I find him and take him into custody."

A change overtook Keepers as she obliged his request. His body tensed. His eyes took on a feverish glow. He toweled her body with his hands.

She recognized she had ignited his passion and used it as her salvation from any lingering suspicions he might have about her.

"Yes, yes," she whispered in his ear, encouragement he didn't need. He threw her onto the bed and didn't bother to completely undress before falling on top of her.

"Yes, yes," she said, louder this time, urging his performance with words like *faster* and *harder* and *deeper.* She pounded on him, called him names, ordered him to fight back.

He slapped her face.

She slapped back.

He grabbed her by the neck, squeezed hard, then harder, too consumed by lust to realize he was squeezing the life out of her.

"What's done is done," Keepers told himself. He spent a brief period mourning his dead wife and developing the story he would use to explain what happened, how he had arrived home to find her on the verge of dying, telling him with her last breaths how she was attacked, beaten, and raped, naming Ruben Garner as her dastardly attacker.

By morning, the story had been widely spread and believed throughout the community.

Keepers left to others the task of arranging a proper funeral. He devoted his time and bankroll to hiring trackers to locate Garner, to see justice served in loving memory of his dear, departed wife.

It didn't take long.

Garner was on the trail to Casa Pleach, the safe haven for desperadoes dodging the long reach of the law.

"I should have figured months ago he

would find safe harbor with that crooked crank of a phony doctor and others of his kind," Keepers said to the tracker who brought him the news. "You're certain it was Garner?"

"Certain, Colonel Keepers. Equally certain I saw the spitting image of Little Tad Logan, who I learned was his twin, Lonely Todd by name, and two others you've mentioned by name, Swaney and McDukes."

"You are certain of this?"

"As sure as the spring follows the winter, sir."

Keepers was elated beyond measure, paid the tracker a handsome bonus, and set about organizing a militia made up of men he could trust, who rode with him or served under him in earlier years. He sent Pronto Leaukomia and Juan Forminfante ahead to scout Casa Pleach while he schooled and drilled the others in the tactics of invasion he planned to utilize.

He visited the grave of his dead wife, laid down a dozen fresh roses, and told her: "It won't be brutal, my love. I only plan to kill."

CHAPTER 20

People started calling Cactus Billy Clemens a crybaby after the love of his life, Jeanne d'Evreaux, was snatched away from Madam Annie's whorehouse in New Testament by Lowell Swaney. Billy didn't mind. He figured picturing him as a broken-hearted, cactus-draining kid kept them from suspecting he was "El Coyote," whose masked exploits robbing stagecoaches and railroads kept readers of the dime weeklies enthralled, a real-life Robin Hood to the Denver Dans and Fancy Franks who lived only on their pages.

Unlike Robin Hood, El Coyote robbed from the rich and kept the spoils for himself.

Not even his mother and father knew the truth. They pictured Billy as the perfect son, an ideal scholar, and a stalwart churchgoing student of the Bible.

Before Jeanne was taken, Billy considered retiring from his double life, settling down to a real life with her. She was worth the price. Afterward, he was consumed by a passion for revenge on Swaney and stayed El Coyote.

Was he good at it?

He was better than good at it.

One of his stagecoach victims, a traveling salesman of long standing who specialized in ladies' undergarments he claimed were imported directly from France, told Frank Leslie, "I have been held up by them all, even the legendary Black Bart, but none ever so professional and polite as El Coyote. He even tended to the needs of a lady passenger, who purchased from me a pair of size twelve, lace-fringed silk bloomers in red and fainted at first sight of his pistol.

"El Coyote made us promise to stay put, hurried away, and returned a few minutes later with a pocket handkerchief soaked in milk he extracted from a nearby cactus and meant for the lady to ingest, promising she would feel a hundred percent better in minutes. She did, too. How's that for knowing your business?"

Without explanation, El Coyote's good deed was attributed by the various weeklies to Black Bart, the Nevada Kid, the Utah Kid, and the Arizona Kid. It was often the same when he held up passengers on a train

coach, his most audacious and lucrative robberies credited to Little Dingus, the outlaw
James boy who worked the rails with his
brother, Frank.

Billy's anger at the disrespect showed him
by the weeklies caused him to write letters
of complaint demanding credit to him
where credit was due, but at the last moment thought better of it and destroyed the
letters. Fame was fine, he decided, but it
was far better that he keep up the good
work, amass enough fortune to ultimately
retire to a comfortable life with Jeanne, once
he found and rescued her.

What altered that plan was a sleepy-eyed
Pinkerton agent on vacation, carefully
studying the selection of sandwiches on the
candy butcher's lunch tray when El Coyote
entered the coach wagging his revolver and
hollering, as if he had invented the concept:
"This is a holdup!"

The Pinkerton let go of the buffalo,
cucumber, and tomato sandwich on home-
made honey bread that had tempted him
and, as he had been trained, without a
moment's hesitation drew the sidearm from
his shoulder holster and commanded:
"Drop it or you're a dead man."

"You," El Coyote said, unflinching.

"I asked first, nice and polite, so don't go

tempting me, Jesse."

"Damn it all to Hell, I ain't Jesse."

"Sure as blazes you are, Jesse. I know my reading matter."

Billy pulled down the bandana hiding half his face. "Do I look like any pictures you seen of Little Dingus?"

"Well I'll be hornswoggled. Not even close, and sure as shit not Frank either. So who are you, young fella?"

"You ever read about El Coyote? That's who I am, the desperado Ned Buntline himself wrote so favorably about, citing me as an up-and-coming *bandito* cut from the same cloth as the Cisco Kid and Zorro." He used his revolver to write a Z in the air.

"First of all, they were on the side of law and order, like us Pinkertons. Second of all, I see now you ain't no Mex, so why do you hide behind some Mex name and make them all look bad? Call yourself *The* Coyote if you got to call yourself anything but your real name. What is your real name? I'd like to know who I'll be taking down if he doesn't drop his gun."

"Not before I drop you," Billy said. He fired. His shot dropped the Pinkerton, whose own shot was late and flew into the ceiling of the coach car. He apologized to the passengers for any inconvenience, withdrew, and hopped off the train as it slowed rounding a bend.

"Damn," he said, tumbling to a safe stop. "I forgot to relieve all them folks of their valuables, too busy defending my good name from that fat-faced galoot trying to pass me off as Jesse."

He set off to find his horse and head on to Casa Pleach, where he was certain to be safe from any Pinkertons hunting for El Coyote.

But not, it turns out, from the two Skinner Gang members who a short time later invaded his campsite. Both Skinners had the hard-boned look of well-practiced cutthroats, especially the one pointing the Winchester at Billy.

The other one said, "Don't mean you no harm, cowboy. Only looking to rest our horses and our own weary bones running from filthy Injuns looking to even the score for all their scalps we been taking."

He sounded as sincere as the Big Bad Wolf knocking on the Three Little Pigs' door. The many scalps dangling from their belts looked nothing like they were of Injun origin. Maybe they were, but Billy was taking no chances. He cocked the .45 he was sleeping with and fired through the blanket.

The Skinner with the Winchester flew

backward and lost his grip on the rifle, too dead to care. The other Skinner caught Billy's next bullet in the throat, leaving unfinished whatever he started to say before he hit the dirt.

"And that's that," Billy said.

He intended to turn over and catch what sleep he could before the dark gave way to daylight when four bare-chested Injun youths wielding bows, tomahawks, and pistols rushed out of the tall grass and surrounded him before he could defend himself. They saw the scalps hanging from the Skinners' horses and talked their Injun talk, glancing down at Billy like he was responsible.

"Only them done it, not me," he said, hoping maybe one of them talked enough English to understand his words. "Them" he said, pointing a forefinger at the dead Skinners. "Not me," he said, shifting his head left and right.

One of the Injuns duplicated Billy's gestures. "Them," he said. "Not me."

"Yes, that's right," Billy said, nodding.

"Yes, that right," the Injun said, nodding, and fired an arrow into Billy, who watched helplessly as they scalped the two Skinners before piling them onto the campfire and, as the flames rose into the frigid night air, did some sort of noisy victory dance, waving their bows, knives, tomahawks, and quirts.

Billy, using his palm to lessen the spill of blood, figured he was next.

The thought knocked him out.

He woke up, unsure how many hours later, wondering if this was Heaven before he saw the four Injuns stretched out dead and Ruben Garner sitting across from him, warming his hands on a cup of java.

Garner smiled and toasted Billy. "Sent them to their happy hunting ground and patched you up," he said. "Another few inches and you would have been dead and gone before I could do you any good at all."

After two more days of rest, they set their sights on Casa Pleach, Cactus Billy Clemens blind to the idea of achieving the showdown he so dearly wanted, Ruben Garner unaware he was heading for a special communion with fate.

Lonely Todd Logan was on Dr. Pleach's porch when Swaney and McDukes arrived at Casa Pleach. He greeted both warmly, although uncertain at first who was which now that the clean-shaven Swaney's bruises and scars were exposed and the battering that altered the appearance of McDukes was buried under a bushel of whiskers hiding his bobbing Adam's apple.

Dr. Pleach stepped out with words of welcome and pointed to the drag cot carrying the bundled, immobile body of Rachel Stump. "What's that all about, boys?" he said.

McDukes said, "Soaring Eagle's squaw gone to rot. I found her on the trail and owed her one, so here she is. I'm ready and able to pay whatever you say to either get her back on her feet or plant her six feet under."

"Fair enough," the doctor said. "From here the squaw don't look like she's getting ready to do any waltzing just yet."

Ned Buchanan, a quiet observer to now, said, "That's for certain."

Swaney said, "Any concerns about Injuns showing up to take her back, Doc?"

"None, not ever. They treat them graves surrounding this place as sacred ground, like they do their own burial grounds. Attacking us would be bad medicine."

Dr. Pleach stepped down to check her out at close range.

He pulled back the blanket on Soaring Eagle's squaw and recoiled, his face drained of color. He shouted once and then again,

"Tell me full how you came upon my daughter."

Alarmed by the nature of her poppa's voice, Katy Pleach ran out of the house and to his side, at once saw the cause, and swooned into a bundle at the foot of the drag cot.

"Quick, help me get her to my exam table," the doctor said. Logan moved to help Katy back onto her feet. "Not her, idiot. My other daughter. My Lucy."

"The squaw's name is Rachel, not Lucy," Swaney said.

"It's Lucille Marie Rachel Pleach. I ought to know the name of my own flesh and blood. Now, please, hurry her into the house."

Katy dragged after them a few minutes later. She saw her father readying to treat her sister, and swooned again.

Dr. Pleach said, "Boys, if you're of a mind to pray, now would be as good a time as any."

"I promise she'll have our best words," Logan said.

"I mean for me," the doctor said. "Pray for me that this dear child of mine does better than her wretched poppa deserves."

Rachel Pleach stirred. As her vision cleared, she realized who was hovering over her, made a painful noise, and fell back unconscious.

Dr. Pleach, his eyes blurred by tears, working by the eerie light of an oil lamp, did what he could to treat her wounds and sustain life in his errant daughter. When he finished, he moved the lamp aside and settled on a straight-backed chair alongside her, monitored her breathing, and mumbled prayers of appeal for her well-being, no longer plagued by the misfortunes that made him banish his daughter from her home and family; cursing Jimmy Stump as the cause.

Jimmy Stump.

A smooth talker that one.

He came into their lives seeking refuge from the law.

He fascinated Rachel from the moment they met, charming her with his tales of derring-do as the Colorado Kid. Most were inventions, but she was too young to know the difference, too much a romantic to believe her poppa when he told her so.

The doctor said, "He's a liar, child, taking credit for exploits the dime weeklies credit to two outlaws named Longabaugh and Parker. I don't believe half his punctuation, much less any of his words. He's leading you down the garden path."

"You are jealous is all, Poppa. Besides, we don't even got a garden," she said, neglecting to mention Jimmy's words she believed the most were *I love you.*

When he caught Jimmy in her bed, the doctor ordered him to leave Casa Pleach.

She begged her poppa to let Jimmy stay.

Pleach saw it as a betrayal, an insolent transfer of affection and loyalty, and told her to leave with Jimmy — go, get out — and never return.

She took his name without benefit of clergy and as further evidence of her new life ceased calling herself "Lucy" and became "Rachel." Eager to please, she joined him in the outlaw trade and proved a quick learner.

Jimmy broke her in slowly.

Posing as weary travelers in need of a hot meal and a bed for the night, whether under roof or in the barn, they'd visit a homestead. Their youth and innocent good looks were rarely turned away by Good Samaritans, who shortly found themselves facing a Winchester and a Colt, stripped of cash and other valuables, and then left hogtied.

Rachel's first encounter with murder came after a few months.

A homesteader, a heavyset man twice Jimmy's size and weight, managed to get free of his ropes, shoved her aside, jumped Jimmy, and wrestled him to the floor.

"Sweetie, shoot him," Jimmy called out.

Without hesitation, she pressed the Colt against the homesteader's temple, and fired.

Jimmy pushed the homesteader's lifeless body aside and pulled Rachel to him. "You saved my life. Are you okay? How do you feel?"

"Saving your life made it easy, sweetie. I will do it again, I ever got to, for the same reason."

"Who could ask for anything more from his girl," Jimmy said.

They made love.

The weeks rolled by.

Jimmy killed once or twice for sport, Rachel once when she felt insulted by the nasty names a farmer's wife was hurling at her.

"It gets easier, don't it, sweetie?" she said, staring down at her victim.

"Like shooting fish in a barrel," Jimmy said. To prove his point, he shot and killed the farmer.

The next victims were an immigrant couple who had sailed to America from the old country in search of a better life.

Jimmy called it their lucky day when he discovered gold coins in a bulging sackcloth bag on the dining table. There were a hundred of them, as well as twenty-odd pieces of silver. They celebrated their good fortune by getting drunk over an unopened bottle of cherry red wine Rachel came across on a cabinet shelf, and woke the next morning to find the cabin overrun by a band of marauding Injuns.

Jimmy knew enough redskin sign language to communicate with their leader, who called himself Soaring Eagle. "See there, gold and silver in the bag," he said. "All yours, you let us go in peace."

"Mine anyway," Soaring Eagle said, devoid of emotion, a hard look burning in his eyes. "What else?"

Fast as a fox, Jimmy faked a smile. "I got something even better we can trade for."

Soaring Eagle crossed his arms over his bare chest and waited to hear him out.

"I'll trade you my woman for my life," Jimmy said.

Soaring Eagle glanced over at Rachel and drank her in with his eyes. His expression seemed to soften.

Jimmy said, "I guarantee you won't regret it. I got her broken in for clean loving and whatever else you might desire, so, mark my words, it's a fair trade."

Rachel said, "What's happening, sweetie?

286

What are you and the Injun carrying on about?"

"Patience, sweetie, the chief here's got a bug up his ass about running off with you. I'm trying my best to get him to change his mind." He renewed his smile. "So, what do you say, Soaring Eagle? How about it? We have a deal then?"

"Mine anyway," Soaring Eagle said as he raised his army issue rifle and pumped a kill shot into Jimmy.

Rachel screamed and started for him.

One of the braves grabbed her, held her kicking and screaming while Soaring Eagle took Jimmy's scalp and two other braves made quick work of skinning him.

Soaring Eagle grinned and took control of Rachel, then told her in slow, imperfect English, "Now you mine."

She knew to argue with him would get her killed. She was too smart to let that happen. It wasn't what Jimmy would want her to do. She said, "Yes, I am."

Dr. Pleach spent hours by Rachel's bed, monitoring her breathing, making sure it never quit on her. He spoke to her in tender terms, as if she could hear him. He urged her to overcome her wounds, allow the healing process to restore bliss and harmony to the family.

He appeared unaware of the toll his attitude was taking on his younger daughter.

Katy resented being shunted aside, always the case before Rachel was sent packing by the filthy old man who masqueraded as a doctor, leaving only Katy to satisfy his lust.

She finally threatened to expose him for the phony doctor he was and always had been, a traveling salesman whose single skill was bilking people. "A real doctor would have my sister well on the road to recovery," she said.

Dr. Pleach disagreed. "Listen, daughter. I'm saying this to you one time only," he said. "Them brought to me are brought for hope as well as survival. That's better than nothing. They live, we all profit. They die, they get the salvation properly due them, no matter what. If I was not here doing the best I can, Lucy would be dead already."

"Maybe a better fate than living under your roof again," Katy said.

She charged out of the room, and the doctor returned his attention to her sister. "Don't mind her one inch," he said. "Katy truly wants you better and us back to being a loving family." He prayed for any saint with healing powers to come down and provide a miracle.

Instead, Dr. Pleach got Ruben Garner and Cactus Billy Clemens.

They raced into Casa Pleach like they were only a few steps ahead of the Red Sea closing up on them. Garner nodded at faces he knew, almost tripped over his own boots when he sighted Lonely Todd Logan, the mirror image of his dead brother, Little Tad.

"We got the likes of an army advancing on our tails, headed by Colonel Frances Milstead Keepers," Garner said.

Cactus Billy, distracted from the danger when he sighted Lowell Swaney, said, "I been hungry for this showdown, Swaney, and no time like the present. Draw."

CHAPTER 21

Swaney refused to draw.

Cactus Billy, full of pepper since Garner nursed him back to health, shouted, "Coward!"

Ned Buchanan said, "Holster your temper, Billy. Aim your rage for now at this Keepers militia heading our way."

Swaney said, "Take his word as gospel, Billy. I'll give you an easy death later, if you so desire, but understand you'll be obliged to get in line." He tossed a knowing look at McDukes, who feigned deafness and tried choking back a brief smile.

Garner digested the scene whole. He was tempted to heap pleasure over seeing McDukes again and in great shape, but held back, figuring such an expression would alienate Swaney. It was more important they work together on a plan to hold off Keepers and his mercenaries.

The plan came together quickly. It wasn't

perfect, but it was better than nothing.

Swaney, McDukes, and Logan took command of the residence in shifts.

Billy was assigned to watch over Dr. Pleach and his two daughters.

Under cover of darkness and benefitting from a moon hiding behind fat, black clouds threatening rain, Garner would sneak away from Casa Pleach in one direction, Buchanan in another.

Billy suffered a relapse from his old wounds, most likely brought on by a severe case of nerves, and fell in need of Dr. Pleach.

The doctor looked him over. "Billy, it appears to me my medication will have you back on your game in twenty-four hours the latest." He told Katy to fetch his basic compounds and tonics.

"We out of Neuralgia King, Poppa. Double Imperial Granum okay?"

"Long as you keep some aside for me in late winter, unless that's already been done with the celery compound."

"You sure this'll help me some?" Billy said, suffering fresh stomach cramps.

"Nobody I ever prescribed the cure for has ever come back and complained afterward," Dr. Pleach said. "That so, Katy?"

"One hundred percent, Poppa."

Billy's cramps eased and he fell asleep during the cure. His snore dropped in volume before it disappeared. He mumbled a single word over and over that became clearer with time. "Jeanne," he said. "Jeanne . . . Jeanne."

Katy said, "He's calling me Jeanne, Poppa. Why do you think?"

"Would not be the first time I seen my cure jumble a wounded body and mind. It don't ever last. He'll know you're a Katy when he snaps out of it," the doctor said.

His explanation wasn't the truth, but it satisfied her.

She continued spoon-feeding Billy celery compound, gently easing the spoon between his parched lips, until her poppa left to take a brief nap and they were alone.

She substituted her lips for the spoon and blended words of reassurance with her kisses.

"You call me Jeanne or however you like, Billy boy, so long as you get better," she said.

She took his hand and guided it to her breasts first, then underneath her petticoat and inside her bloomers.

"My cure for what ails you, Billy boy," she said.

Billy turned on his side calling out for

Jeanne before abruptly raising his voice in anger. "Bastard Swaney, get ready to die," he said. "You stole my woman, my Jeanne, and I intend to end your miserable life."

Katy snapped her hand back.

Whoever Jeanne was, Billy didn't have Katy in mind.

Frustrated and angry with herself, she went looking for Lonely Todd. He was napping, not yet due to begin his shift.

She crawled into bed beside him and prodded him awake.

Lonely Todd said, "I been waiting for you, darling one."

"Wait's over," Katy said.

Two days later, before the bullet whizzed out of nowhere and came close to corking an eye socket, Lonely Todd Logan was on the veranda sharing memories of his brother, Little Tad, with Ruben Garner. Garner had finally overcome his reluctance to tell him Little Tad was dead and describe what he knew of Colonel Francis Milstead Keepers's involvement.

Lonely Todd exhibited scant emotion accepting Garner's news. Only a quiver in his voice betrayed the sadness he tried to hide by smiling his way through tales about all their happy times together.

Garner pulled out a hip flask. "Here's to your brother," he said; then took a healthy swallow and handed the flask to Lonely Todd.

"To Tad," Lonely Todd said. "I always figured I would beat you to the finish line, but you won again, damn it, little runt that you are."

They drank more than they spoke for a while, until Logan trimmed away the silence with talk of Colonel Keepers. "Was a bleak period in my life. I was obliged to toady for that military pig fucker," he said. "Being in his debt put me in his keep, and I longed for the day I could break away. It finally come my way in the company of a cowboy I thought to be McDukes, who turned out to be Swaney, or so I learned later from Ned Buchanan."

The story Logan recited, years later expanded upon by certain of the dime weeklies, had Colonel Keepers fearing the arrival in Atonement by Swaney and McDukes, who owned secrets from a past he had worked diligently to bury. He believed they had come to kill him, but that was not the case. Both had suffered memory loss and had no awareness of Keepers in their past.

Logan said, "Things was peaceful at first, until the colonel learned they was living with an Injun squaw name of Flowing Beaver. That got his jelly beans jumping. He wasn't allowing Swaney and McDukes to set a bad example for other white men. He got crazier and crazier on the subject and set about correcting it for good and final. He tells me, 'After all this time, the one what swore revenge still travels with the one he means to kill, and that's not even the biggest jest of all. I'm the one what killed McDukes's wife and should suffer his anger, not that scout bastard Swaney.' "

Garner said, "You think word got back to McDukes, and that's how come Swaney still lives anymore?"

"Possible, same way that parcel of information and more could have reached Ruben Garner during your time in Atonement."

"Me? What's that supposed to mean?" Garner said, surprised to hear his name cited.

"Heard about you from my brother, how, when you come to town, you went around asking lots of questions about the colonel's past and how the colonel's wife might of been playing around with McDukes behind the colonel's back before she was killed."

"I was on a tracking mission for McDukes. It was at a time we were partners."

"You say so, fine by me." Logan paused to

295

roll and light a Bull Durham.

That's when the shot narrowly missed him.

Logan yowled and dove over the veranda railing to the lawn.

Another shot caused Garner to tumble backward over the railing.

Two more shots rang out.

Garner bellied up to the front door, Logan not far behind.

Shots flew by them.

The door opened a crack.

"No," Garner yelled. "Cut them lights first."

Casa Pleach went dark.

The door opened wide enough for McDukes to get Garner and Logan inside before he yanked it shut and Swaney dropped the safety bar.

Two shots slammed into the door.

Everyone flattened out on the floor.

"What do you suppose?" McDukes said. "Is it the colonel already?"

"Bandits, maybe, but this ain't their way of doing things," Logan said, "so the colonel is as good a bet as any."

McDukes said, "If that's true, him and his people wasted no time getting here. Wouldn't you say so, Rube?"

No reply.

"Rube, you hear me?"

No reply.

"Ruben, you okay, or did you catch a bullet?"

In fact, Garner was gone.

In those early minutes of darkness, he had somehow managed to slip away.

Dr. Pleach broke his silence, complaining, "I refuse to allow a gun battle on my premises. This is a house of healing, not a house of carnage."

He lit his oil lamp.

A bullet crashed through a window opening and just missed him.

Swaney said, "Turn off the damn light, Doc."

"This house is my house and I make all the decisions, not you or any of you."

Swaney moved on Pleach and jammed his Colt into the doctor's rib cage. "My gun says otherwise, Doc. Turn off the damn light."

Pleach was unyielding. "Go ahead and shoot, Swaney, for it's to be my way or no way."

Billy crossed the room and used the handle of his revolver to conk Dr. Pleach on the noggin. Swaney got control of the lamp and extinguished the flame before the doctor landed unconscious to the floor.

"And that's that," Billy said.

McDukes said, "While you boys was having your fun, you notice the shooting stopped?"

"Garner's doing, or maybe Buchanan?" Logan said.

"Could be either," Swaney said.

"Or neither," McDukes said.

"What do we do now?" Billy said.

"We wait," McDukes said.

The shooters were Pronto Leaukomia and Juan Forminfante, who were not supposed to fire, only scout Casa Pleach and report back to Colonel Keepers.

Forminfante's trigger finger got the best of him when he spotted Lonely Todd Logan and mistook him for his brother, Little Tad, whom he believed dead already.

The shot revealed their presence, obliging them to continue firing, keeping everyone pinned down until Keepers and his militia arrived.

Garner tracked the sounds and the brief flashes of gunfire light after slipping away from the casa. He got Leaukomia in his sights, aimed, and fired. The shot caught Leaukomia's horse. It fell, pinning Leaukomia underneath. Garner's aim was truer with the next shots. He got Forminfante between the shoulders, in the small of the back, and in the neck. In doing so, Garner fell off his horse, which trotted away.

Garner raced after Leaukomia, but Leaukomia had managed to free himself from the dead animal and disappear into the thickets.

Garner found Forminfante minutes away from dying.

"Kill me," Forminfante said, as close to begging as Garner ever heard. "Put another bullet in me and finish the job you began."

"You ain't getting off so easy," Garner said. He took his Bowie from inside his belt. "I owe you for what you done to a pal of mine, Little Tad Logan by name."

He proceeded to take Forminfante's scalp and cut off Forminfante's right hand.

"One for me and one for you, Little Tad," Garner called to the sky. "And you, Forminfante, I hope you are still alive to recognize my joy."

He jammed a boot into Forminfante, got no response.

"Damn," he said.

Garner wrapped the hand and scalp inside a blanket and packed it in his saddlebag before riding off, leaving Forminfante's remains to the buzzards and four-legged scavengers.

"One escaped from us tonight," he said, as if Logan were riding alongside him, "but I still got me plenty time and patience working for us, Little Tad."

Leaukomia owed someone for the broken ankle he suffered under his horse's weight, so he was not about to head back to Colonel Keepers without first getting even. He limped to the casa, careful not to be observed, and climbed inside through an unsecured window, to an unlit room he sensed was empty.

The sound of even breathing informed him otherwise.

He followed the sound to the side of a bed, but was unable to discern whether it was a man or a woman, much less Rachel Stump, too deep in sleep to be disturbed by intruder noises.

The sound of somebody outside the door, his muffled words saying, "I'll check on her and be right back," caused Leaukomia to hurry away from the bed.

The door opened and Dr. Pleach slipped inside the room, bringing with him the eerie orange glow of his oil lamp.

Moving quickly, Leaukomia grabbed Dr. Pleach from behind, clamped a hand over his mouth, and dug the inside of his elbow against the doctor's throat, taking control of the oil lamp while choking Pleach to death.

Rachel Stump, near death herself, roused long enough to observe her father's murder. She opened her mouth to call for help, but words failed her. She fell back asleep.

Leaukomia eased the doctor's body onto the floor and rolled it out of the way before he returned his attention to the woman. "Let's me and you have ourselves some fun," he said, like a reckless dog in heat.

He dropped his britches, threw back the covers, and fell on top of her.

He was grunting within seconds.

Bare seconds later, her breathing grew heavier, induced by the stimulation. She wrapped her muscular legs over Leaukomia. Locked them at the ankles. Bounced spasmodically. Gasped a single word that sounded to him like *Poppa.*

It was another minute before Leaukomia recognized Rachel wasn't breathing.

He put an ear to her nose and then to her mouth, but heard nothing.

Rachel was dead.

Leaukomia couldn't move off her.

Her legs had him trapped.

He tried to remain calm, telling himself, "Don't panic, Pronto. Take your time and you will be free from this bitch before you know. She was not so hot stuff anyway. You give her a real treat, so that's a good deed on you, *amigo*. You listening, bitch? I done you a favor for a goodbye present."

Concerned by the long absence of her father, Katy excused herself to check on him.

She entered her sister's room and yelled for help, alarmed by the sight of Dr. Pleach on the floor and someone stretched out on top of Rachel.

Lonely Todd, Billy, and McDukes came running, followed by Swaney.

Katy fell to her knees alongside the doctor, in a frenzy, trying to shake her father back from the dead. Billy at her side was unable to calm her.

Swaney joined McDukes in dragging Leaukomia off the bed and roping him to a chair.

Lonely Todd broke his somber silence to tell them, "Leaukomia is mine, for what he done to my brother, Tad. I'm claiming him in the name of frontier justice."

Billy helped Katy to her feet. "And me twice as much as you," she said. "Look around and I don't need to explain no further."

Hearing no argument to her claim, she

left the room and was back in minutes toting her father's medical satchel. She turned it over to Logan, who located a thin, stainless steel scalpel, tested its sharpness by halving a lock of his hair, and deemed it suitable for his intention.

He stepped over to Leaukomia and invited Katy to join him.

She staked a position behind Leaukomia, took a handful of his long and greasy black hair, and used it to pull back his head.

"How's that, Logan?" she said.

He nodded approval. "You got any last words, Leaukomia?"

"Do what you got to do."

"That's my intention and them's your last words."

He forced open Leaukomia's mouth, pulled out his tongue, and with one swift slash cut it off. Katy shoved his head forward to prevent him from choking to death on his own blood. The blood trickled over his lips and onto his buckskin vest and bare legs. Logan handed her the tongue and offered her the scalpel.

"You got need for more, now's the time, Katy."

She took the blade; at first she seemed uncertain what she was doing with it, but only for a minute before she jammed the scalpel through his lid into his left eye. She left it there, dropped the severed tongue, and fled the room.

Logan chased after her.

The room was empty when Leaukomia opened his good eye. He had passed out, for how long he didn't know. He was surprised to be alive. He struggled free of his bonds and, armed with the blade he pulled from his dead eye, he went searching for revenge, only to discover he was alone in Casa Pleach.

There was nobody around, not even Dr. Pleach or Rachel.

Their bodies were gone.

Lonely Todd Logan was gone.

Katy Pleach was gone.

Cactus Billy Clemens was gone.

Lowell Swaney was gone.

McDukes was gone.

The story detailed by all the dime weeklies in graphic words and illustrations credited Leaukomia's survival to his brute strength and explained how he stumbled through the casa twice before he heard gunshots and Colonel Keepers saying, "Come out with your hands up or we kill you one and all. This is your only warning and your only chance for surviving."

His voice gone along with his tongue, Leaukomia had the presence of mind to fashion a white flag of surrender using a lace tablecloth tied to a broom handle.

Waving it furiously, he came through the door and was met by a hail of bullets that gave him the death Logan and Katy didn't provide. Colonel Keepers was never one to ever hold truck with surrender, which he outwardly considered the province of cowards.

He and his militia stormed Casa Pleach primed for battle.

There was none to be had.

The casa was empty, well-fed horses in the stable the only evidence anybody besides Leaukomia had been there lately. Had the chase after Swaney and McDukes, and Garner, too, been a fool's mission? The colonel blamed Leaukomia. "The damn fool got what he deserved," he said.

Later, he and his men were hardly encamped indoors when the booming voice of Heck Jarman called from outside, "Keepers, you and your boys stretch on out here with your hands grabbing clouds or we'll burn you out with hot lead."

The colonel ran to a window.

"Heck Jarman, that you?"

"One and the same, Keepers. You plan on

305

heeding good advice?"

"I'll see you in Hell first, Jarman."

"Not if I see you first, Keepers."

Within the hour, bullets were flying back and forth.

CHAPTER 22

The gun battle seemed to be a standoff the first hours, before the pace slowed down to conserve bullets.

A time or two Colonel Keepers called out to Heck Jarman, suggesting peace talks, but Jarman wasn't interested and didn't bother answering him. "I finally got the miserable bastard where I want him," he told Ned Buchanan.

Buchanan had tracked down Jarman and his gang after sneaking away from Casa Pleach, with hopes of enlisting him in a showdown with Keepers and his militia by reporting about their mutual friends and describing the brutal murder of Little Tad Logan.

Jarman's acceptance was immediate, surprising Buchanan.

"Seems like you got your own personal score to settle with him, Heck," Buchanan said. "What's that about?"

"You ever hear tell about the colonel's black hole back during his command days at Fort Bloomer? Twenty feet deep, fourteen more feet than what's expected of grave diggers."

"Lots of times. Ugly punishment for the slightest offense. Lots of prisoners never come up alive."

"That's the place. Keepers give me a two-month whiff of that deadly paradise, because I dared smile back at his lady one day he had her visiting. A smile done that, the only one he ever caught on my face afterward. All these years, I been saving the big one for him to see comes the day I make him my prisoner. I'm in your debt for bringing me that opportunity, Ned."

Jarman and his gang were saddled and on the trail to Casa Pleach as fast as he could bark orders, Buchanan showing them the way.

Jarman waited for darkness before he had some of his boys set aside their carbines and attach strips of cloth to stone-cut arrowheads after soaking the cloth in cans of kerosene. The arrows were set on fire and shot at Casa Pleach.

The casa was soon ablaze beyond redemption. Keepers's mercenaries staggered out

half-blind, choking on smoke. Sharpshooters picked them off one by one, ignoring
pleas for mercy.

Jarman waited for daylight before he
toured the courtyard littered with corpses.

Colonel Keepers was not among them.

Neither were the people Buchanan had
set out to save from Keepers.

They were where Dr. Pleach years earlier
had taught Katy to hide in the event of
danger, in the root cellar where the doctor,
working alone and secretly over many
months, had fashioned a dozen hiding
spaces. Each was twice the size of a burial
plot, shaped in concrete and covered by lids
that blended perfectly with the dirt floor.
Each contained two canteens of water,
several tins of food, and a blanket. Fresh air
was provided through barely noticeable air
holes that easily passed for gopher holes.

Swaney, McDukes, and the others retreated to spaces assigned by Katy at the
first sounds of Colonel Keepers arriving
with his militia. She pulled each lid shut
and, in her hurry, wound up sharing a space
with Lonely Todd Logan.

Following his run-in with Forminfante and
Leaukomia, Ruben Garner tracked after
Heck Jarman to make sure he knew about

the hiding places in the root cellar. He got a warm greeting from Jarman and Buchanan, and joined them for a hot meal around the campfire before preparing to leave.

Buchanan said, "You sure you won't stick around and join us in seeing this to the finish, Rube?"

Jarman said, "Not like you to step away from a battle, Rube."

Garner said, "Nothing ever like a good fight to get my blood boiling, gents, except for the siren's call of a woman, like I been hearing loud and clear since me and her took our last ride on the merry-go-round."

"Who might that be?" Buchanan said.

"A gentleman never tells, Ned," Garner said, figuring he wasn't obliged to reveal it was the colonel's wife he had in mind.

"That lets you out," Jarman said, chuckling at his wisecrack.

Buchanan said, "It must be someone you find yourself unable to resist making your own, like it was for you with Ellie McDukes, bless her soul."

Garner said, "I don't know what you mean, Ned. I don't understand you at all."

"That look on your face tells me you do, Rube. You need help remembering?"

"Try me."

"I talk of Ellie's last walk in the garden

and your sick encounter with her. Now do you get my meaning?"

Garner digested the implication in Buchanan's words, dismissing it with a sweeping hand gesture. "I wasn't there that awful night, Ned. I was off hunting with McDukes. You know that from McDukes himself."

"I also know you made up some excuse to leave him early. McDukes told me so while he was still outside his mind, but gave it no importance. He had already settled on Swaney as guilty, given the lie he was spoon-fed by Keepers."

"Watch what words come from your mouth next, Ned."

"Already said enough, Rube, maybe too much. You live with the truth day in and day out, so you don't need me to remind you any."

Garner's eyes reduced to an ugly squint and his hand hovered over his holster.

Buchanan didn't flinch.

Jarman warned Garner off with a look.

Garner relaxed. "Don't care to keep my woman waiting longer than necessary," he said, and turned to go. "See you around, Ned. The country ain't so big we won't ever again hear each other's hoofbeats."

■ ■ ■ ■

The flames were close to totally devouring Casa Pleach when Colonel Keepers, trapped inside by the gunfire from Jarman's sharpshooters, fled down to the smoke-filled root cellar and stumbled about looking for some way out to safety or a safe hiding place

The colonel tripped, fell into the open hiding space Katy intended for herself before she wound up sharing Logan's space, and broke his neck.

Jarman and Buchanan found him there after the casa had been reduced to rubble and they cleared a path down to the cellar Garner had told them about.

"Keepers looks dead to me," Jarman said. "He look dead to you, Ned?"

"Either that or he's a better actor I ever give him credit for being."

"Bad news to the bitter end, depriving me of the chance to give him the ugly death he deserved." Jarman aimed his Winchester down the hole, and got off three quick shots. "Just to be sure," he said, and offered the rifle to Buchanan.

Buchanan took it gladly. "This one's for Ellie McDukes," he said, and fired.

Jarman called: "Everybody, listen up.

You're safe to come on out now. It's me, Heck Jarman, and I got Ned Buchanan with me."

Everyone but Lonely Todd Logan and Katy Pleach emerged, eyes bloodshot and grateful to be sucking up fresher air.

McDukes called for them, but got no response.

Neither did Swaney.

"I'm thinking I know maybe why," Billy said, pointing to a hiding place barely visible under heavy sections of flooring that caved down and made the lids impossible to push open.

The dime weeklies told the story of Katy and Lonely Todd many times afterward, as if they had been witness to what happened. There were variations, imaginations run rampant, but the stories usually began with Katy settling alongside Logan in his hideout and telling him —

"Todd, I got a confession to make. It was no accident that caused me to get in here with you. I got scared to be alone by myself and you were my first and only choice for company."

"I got that same feeling," Logan said, "and no one I'd rather be spending time with."

"You mean it?"

"I'll let you in on a secret. When this business finished I was intending to ask permission to keep you company."

"That's real sweet of you to say so, even if you don't mean it."

"I do mean it, Katy. You think you would have been agreeable?"

"Still am, Todd." She leaned over and kissed his nose, then his cheek, then his lips.

They shared a warm embrace, his arm wrapped around her, and settled into blissful silence while the noise of battle resounded above, then turned to quiet, and finally to the unmistakable sound and smell of fire.

"They're burning down my home," Katy said, and broke into tears.

Logan held her tighter. "What's got built once can always get built again."

"You'd do that for me?"

"Surely would."

"How about for us? Would you do that for us?"

His smile was all the answer she needed.

Katy and Logan shared hungry kisses and, awkward as the space was, managed to make love.

They were resting in each other's arms when they heard the thud of falling timber above them, followed in minutes by their air

314

beginning to turn stale.

Logan knew at once something had happened to block the air holes. "We need to get out from here while the getting is good," he said.

Katy handed him the pole meant to push open the lid.

The lid budged five or six inches before the pole broke in two and the lid slammed shut.

"It's down to you and me now," Logan said.

He lifted Katy onto his shoulders, giving them sufficient height to reach the lid.

Katy pushed hard.

The lid rose about a foot before slamming shut.

She toppled from his shoulders.

They reversed positions, Logan on Katy's shoulders, in one last, desperate attempt to raise the lid and escape from there.

The attempt failed.

The stale air supply was dwindling, what there was of it accompanied by more and more smoke vapors.

They clutched each other for comfort and traded kisses, made small talk, and pretended a miracle was on the way to rescue them from certain death.

Katy said, "Todd, I never got to go east

like my poppa promised me, and me wanting to see some of the things I only heard about, like tall buildings and electricity and a zoo filled with animals from faraway places all over the world."

"Soon, dear Katy, soon you'll see those things and even more wonders coming."

"You promise me, Todd?"

"I promise, Katy." He brushed away her tears with an index finger, kissed both her eyes, and moved his lips down her cheek and over to her mouth.

"You'll come with me?"

"You bet," he said, easing her closer to him.

"How about Heaven, Todd? You wonder if we'll get to see Heaven together?"

No response.

She repeated the question.

He was beyond answering.

When the lid was lifted and set aside, Katy and Logan were discovered locked in each other's arms, like two lovers caught by surprise.

They were buried that way, together, in a simple grave, under a cross fashioned of twigs and a wood marker carved with their names, date of death, and the message "True Love Lives Here."

■ ■ ■ ■

Katy's father and sister were buried in adjacent graves that limited the markers to their names and date of death, no messages, because nobody could think of anything appropriate to say.

Heck Jarman ordered his boys to bury everyone who died in battle, except the colonel, insisting Keepers be left as buzzard bait, as payment for services rendered.

Billy said, "Kinda cruel that, wouldn't you say so, Heck?"

"It's a cruel world, kid. Keep that in mind and you'll add years to your life away from Boot Hill."

After Jarman said his goodbyes and melted into the horizon with his gang, Buchanan said, "Nothing to keep us here, so anybody got ideas?"

"That town where Swaney got them land leases, where was that again?" McDukes said.

Buchanan said, "Tap Dance by name, and there could be somebody already there worth looking up."

"If you mean a certain lady, sure, Tap Dance. I'm anxious to find a good lady like that, not for me so much as for Swaney here."

Swaney caught the meaning under his words. He said, "I'm for it, if only to keep you in my sights, and take my word for it, McDukes — that day is coming."

"One day, sure, but until then you're better company than any other saddle mate I ever had. How about you, Ned?"

"I'll string along," Buchanan said.

That left only Billy to announce his intention.

He studied the three cowpokes, mostly Swaney, remembering how Swaney stole Jeanne d'Evreaux from him. "No, sir," he said. "I got me some unfinished business here and now with him there, and you know why that come to be, McDukes. I trust you not to get in the way." His gun hand hovered over his holster.

McDukes's hands moved to his twin Frontiers.

Buchanan stepped out of firing range.

McDukes said, "Do yourself a future and bend away from that decision, Billy. He don't go now and for damn sure he don't go a way you choose." The glint in his eye dressed the steel in his voice.

Billy appeared unimpressed by McDukes's reputation. "Believe me when I say, if I choose to drop him what thieved my lady Jeanne from me, I'm ready to dispense with you as well, you try getting in my way, McDukes."

"Don't speak poison you can't translate into a winning hand against me, Billy." McDukes's hands hovered over his holsters.

Billy was resolute. "Swaney deserves to die," he said.

"You get no argument from me. I got my own disagreement with Swaney that needs resolving, but in a way I choose and not today, not here, and not because you say so. Leave Swaney to me as payback for the time I saved your skin out on the open range."

Swaney called to no one in particular, "Glad I got to be so damn popular."

Billy relented. "This makes us even then, but only for today. No guarantee on what the future brings."

"I'll settle for that," McDukes said, and relaxed his hands.

Billy whipped out his gun. "No funny moves, McDukes. I just fooled you with one of the oldest tricks in the book."

"The lying cowards' handbook? A fair showdown wouldn't serve you at all against me."

"Like they say, 'Practice makes perfect.' I'm better with shooting irons now than you

319

ever knew."

"Doesn't matter. I'm the best there is."

"Not better'n me, McDukes," Swaney said.

"Shut up, Swaney."

"You shut up."

"You both shut up," Billy said. He cracked a lopsided grin, twirled the gun around his trigger finger, and dropped it into his holster. "Needed to make a point my way, McDukes. We're good for now, you got my word."

"We're good," McDukes said, "except for one thing."

"Being?"

McDukes drew his Frontiers. "How's that for speed, Billy? Faster'n you. Faster'n him, wasn't it, Buchanan?"

"Looked to be, McDukes."

"I would have been even faster," Swaney said.

McDukes said, "Shut up, Swaney. Don't make me change my mind about not giving you over to Billy and washing my hands of your memory."

Billy said, "You got the drop on me, McDukes, so what now?"

"Just to make my own point, Billy. A real showdown between us and all you would have heard after was the sound of silence."

He holstered the Colts.

"Some other time then."

"I hope not. On my honor and in your best interest, that's the truth."

"I leave it unfinished business for another time." Billy mounted his Pinto and raced down the trail without so much as a goodbye wave.

Swaney said, "Billy whacking me could of saved you the need, McDukes."

"You would have whacked him for certain, so figure me for a saint on your lucky day."

Swaney dropped his smile. "I didn't kill Ellie, McDukes, no matter what you were made to believe."

"Save that tune for somebody drinks lies for liquor."

Buchanan sensed temperatures rising and stepped in. "Do we or don't we head west for Tap Dance, you two? I hear it's still fresh land there, lots more for the taking than what already belongs to you, Swaney. A desert paradise that blooms with greenery and growth twelve months out of the year, fit for any mountain buffer, yet right as rain for any cowman, sheep farmer, sodbuster, and merchant. So, what do you say?"

Swaney said, "Sounds like you're taking over for the late Dr. Pleach selling his Miracle Tonic colored water, Ned."

"What the hell," McDukes said. "We decide the old-fashioned way who picks our trail." He dug a coin from his pocket and tossed it high into the air. It landed heads, the way Swaney called it. "Damn, Swaney. I believe that's the first time ever you won the flip."

"I feel in my bones it won't be the last time, McDukes." He pointed a direction.

"I read that as east. Tap Dance is over west, that other way."

"I know," Swaney answered. He climbed onto his mustang, charged the horse with his spurs, and headed off.

McDukes said, "Can you believe that saddle tramp, Buchanan? I'll surely enjoy killing him comes the day." He hopped onto his horse and put spurs to the gallop after Swaney.

Buchanan followed close behind, wondering how and when it would end between them, not daring to predict the outcome.

CHAPTER 23

Where life suffers beginnings and ends, history is defined by middles.

Not every tale can tidy up the complete story about its people, especially not after the passage of so many years, not even those where I blended fact and fantasy in the dime weekly I come to write for *Old West Tales Tall and True.*

I'm obliged to give it a try, though, and as satisfactory a place as any to start would be with Cactus Billy Clemens, who never achieved his showdown with Swaney or McDukes.

It wasn't that Billy gave up on the idea, only that his calling kept interfering and, finally, got in the way forever.

Billy went back to holding up stagecoaches and trains as El Coyote and made a success of it before he was undone by what's known as a "quirk of fate."

He had maneuvered from his Pinto into a

baggage car said to be transporting thousands in gold, silver, diamonds, and folding cash. He bound and gagged the trainman, unaware he was being observed through the coach window by a wireless operator in the next car.

The operator wasted no time tapping out an urgent warning to the upcoming town on the rail route.

The town marshal and his deputies were ready to capture El Coyote when the train chugged into the station. They couldn't find him on board, figured he had managed to make a clean getaway, and were close to quitting the search.

In fact, he was still on the train.

El Coyote had locked himself in a Pullman compartment washroom, where he altered his appearance with the false goatee, hairpiece, and steel-rimmed spectacles he carried in his loot satchel. Emerging, he eased into an unoccupied seat and relaxed, expecting to easily lose himself among departing passengers at the next stop, a brazen trick that had served him well many times before.

A noisy brat proved his undoing.

The kid, maybe five or six years of age and indulged by his folks, was making a noisy nuisance of himself running up and down the aisle, pretending to be a choo-choo train. Billy, annoyed after too many minutes of this behavior, grabbed the kid by the arm to stop him in his tracks and threatened him with a spanking if he didn't sit down.

The kid wasn't intimidated by Billy's whispered menace. "You not my pops," he yelled as he stuck out his tongue, grabbed at Billy's goatee, and yanked it off, exposing his true identity. The kid's father, a muscular sodbuster twice Billy's size, recognized El Coyote from wanted posters. He clamped onto Billy, wrestled him to the floor, and called out for someone to bring back the lawmen who earlier had passed through the coach.

Justice was swift and unforgiving.

Billy wound up sentenced to years that would turn him into an old man before he tasted freedom again and sent to Keepers Prison, a facility named in honor of a former military leader and pride of the regiment, Colonel Francis Milstead Keepers, barely remembered in this day and age. Billy made light of the sentence at first, spending much of his time in the prison galley teaching other convicts how to milk cacti in order to earn their respect, admiration, and friendship.

Eventually, his thoughts about the innocent pleasures enjoyed by Cactus Billy Clemens in the years before he turned outlaw weren't enough to prevent him from turning despondent. He fashioned a rope from strips of bed sheet, kissed the faded heart on his cell wall proclaiming Billy + Jeanne, and hanged himself. His grave in the prison courtyard was marked by a giant saguaro.

Ruben Garner?

Some had it that Garner died at a poker table, shot in the head by a sore loser named Hap Woosher, who in turn was sought out and killed by Garner's distraught lover, Polly Annie, who afterward turned the six-shooter on herself.

The story was taken as truth and handed down over the years, until a saggy-skinned gent approaching old age stepped forward, claiming he was that selfsame Ruben Garner. He spun one fancy tale after another that drew him as a hero of epic stature, all eventually retold in a boastful ghostwritten autobiography titled *Rube Garner: Lord of the Wild Frontier.*

Some chapters spoke about his encounters with Swaney and McDukes, the best known of the saddle mates who roamed the Old

West. The chapters were later turned into a moving picture where the three shared adventures that routinely had Garner saving Swaney and McDukes from certain death or disaster. It made for a good movie, if not a good truth, and turned Garner into a rich man.

Some years before he died, when the question of his true identity burned brightest, dime weekly historians arranged a face-to-face confrontation between the self-proclaimed Garner and cowboy icon Bat Masterson, who quit helping tame the West to become a reporter and columnist with the *New York Morning Telegraph.*

Masterson only needed minutes of observation to declare, "I crossed paths with Ruben Garner many a time when I was a lawman and say without hesitation that I don't know who this fellow is, but he is not Ruben Garner."

Garner dismissed Masterson's declaration as the conclusion of an old codger with bad eyesight and a worse memory. "Besides which, he was not the Bat Masterson I ever knew," he said. "That Bat Masterson went down in a hail of Clanton bullets when he joined up with Wyatt at the O.K. Corral."

"I was not at that gunfight, you dang fool."

"That's what I'm saying. You wasn't, but

Bat Masterson, he were, so you got no business making light of me."

"You have me confused with Doc Holliday. Doc was there, not me."

"I know Holliday myself. He pulled an infected tooth from my choppers one time. He were around, he would set your lying eyes straight about me and who I am."

They carried on like that for several minutes before Masterson threw up his hands and fled after announcing he intended to describe Garner as a fraud in his column.

A few days later, he was found slumped over his typewriter in the *Telegraph* city room, dead from a heart attack.

Contacted for a quote, Garner said, "He meant to write about me and how I helped out winning the West."

None of the historians who had brought him together with Masterson thought to dispute or correct Garner's remark. In time, it took on the veneer of truth, as it stands to this day.

Jeanne d'Evreaux?

She made it to Tap Dance with an infant child, accompanied by a limping Injun squaw and not yet recovered from the tragic loss of her man, Dr. Marion Wilson Beverage. Versions of how she met the Injun differed. Common gossip suggested the squaw found her isolated in a cabin while on the hunt for a lying scoundrel named Harvey Winslow, who promised to restore her severed toe in trade for a deed to Tap Dance acres.

Jeanne was in labor. The squaw, whose name was Flowing Beaver, guided her through the worst of a painful delivery; a healthy boy fair of hair and complexion, eyes blacker than coal, all fingers and toes accounted for, a lusty cry that would cause many a sleepless night.

When Jeanne was up for conversation, Flowing Beaver, asked her, "What you name?"

"Jeanne," she said, misunderstanding the question.

Flowing Beaver misunderstood the answer and thereafter called the child "Jon."

When Jeanne and Jon were strong enough to travel, the Injun said, "We go now."

"How?" Jeanne said.

"Hello?" Flowing Beaver said.

The trail to Tap Dance was difficult to follow, but they arrived without incident and settled into an abandoned shack on government-granted Injun land bordering the town.

Jeanne rarely ventured into Tap Dance, choosing to spend her days on the reservation. She taught the children in a one-room schoolhouse, became a beloved lady of the land, and the first paleface to be voted a seat on the tribal council. Flowing Beaver was always there with loving support. Jon d'Evreaux grew up tall and strong and years later rode off to win a just and proper fame that carried him to the highest levels of government.

Flowing Beaver never got her toe back, but she did achieve revenge on Harvey Winslow. It happened unexpectedly, soon after she observed him riding along the main street of Tap Dance and took her story to the tribal chief of the reservation, an old, white-haired survivor of the Plains, now given to curious memories and odious warts.

Some said he was Soaring Eagle.

Others called him Sitting Bull.

Geronimo or Black Kettle?

Maybe Chief Joseph?

This chief took whatever name was offered and never volunteered otherwise.

Flowing Beaver waited patiently to hear back from him.

He summoned her after four days to his modest lodge, newly decorated with a dangling parcel of hair nailed to a wall.

"It is done, daughter," he said, "all thanks to Corvis, mighty god of good hunting."

Harvey Whiting was never again seen riding the streets of Tap Dance, or anywhere.

It was years before I heard the end of that story and discovered the land leases Flowing Beaver coveted were no longer valid, now no more than another piece of history illustrating our government's unfair treatment of the Injun nation.

This was on my second visit to Tap Dance, a town destined for growth and prosperity, thanks largely to the hundreds of laborers who laid water pipe through the arid desert clime and unintentionally gave Tap Dance its name. After connecting one section of pipe to the next, they would climb on top, turn the valves that released water into the system, and tap out a rhythmic victory dance.

I could have retired there, I suppose, having enjoyed more than a fair share of adventure by myself and with Swaney and McDukes, but I was not yet ready to take to a rocking chair, not as long as I could fill my time researching and writing for *Old West Tales Tall and True.*

I was on a research mission, looking to check some history against the truth, again

331

capture the reality of past times before the vanishing prairie lost its last battles against a civilization growing rich with motor cars, factories, tall buildings, and bright lights.

Tap Dance.

It was a name that would stick, unlike so many that would fold into memory for places like First Refusal, Atonement, Heads High, Scuffers Meadow, Pentameter, Lonely Vigil, and New Testament. There would always be gangs, of course, none as colorful as the Padrones, the Skunkers, or the Wandering Jutes, few if any with charismatic leaders like Heck Jarman.

I saw Heck ever so often, when I was up Washington way.

He would dash out of chambers like urgent business required his attention and guide me to his office, to enjoy a smoke and a few swigs from his hip flask. We would trade stories from our past and marvel how we'd managed to live long enough to share them. I'd always part with him telling me, "You ever need help for any reason at all, don't hesitate."

The government threw him a princely state funeral when he breathed his last from what they were calling the "Big C." A lot of people in suits and ties took to the podium to describe Heck in generous terms, trying

332

hard to sound like they knew him. Not one familiar face in the bunch. They didn't know him. I knew him. I kept our stories to myself. They were never meant to be shared.

Peggy Elizabeth Terry was behind my second visit to Tap Dance. She had been brought to my attention by Jon d'Evreaux, who was engaged to her daughter. She was an elegant lady of rare beauty, who burst into tears when our conversation over tea and dessert cookies caught up with the name McDukes.

Her husband, the town mayor, said, "Peg, how is it you fret like that?"

She said nothing

Neither did I.

He appeared to understand her silence and left us to ourselves.

We resumed quoting private nuggets of history back and forth for hours that passed like seconds.

I parted from her, envious over any man who could keep so fine a bonfire as Peg Terry so brightly stoked for so many decades.

Like McDukes.

Or was it Lowell Swaney who had captured her life?

Jon had one more visit in mind for me,

nothing he mentioned earlier.

I climbed into his buggy and he drove us onto the reservation, to his mother's home.

"I didn't say you'd be coming, so it will be a welcome surprise for her," he said, failing to mention Jeanne was caught up in some pox that clutched at her body with no intention of ever letting go. She was dying.

She and I had stayed in touch over the years, so I knew Flowing Beaver died some time ago, along with the old chief.

Now it was Jeanne's turn.

I walked to her bedside, took her limp hand in mine, and gave it a gentle kiss. "Hey, kid, you remember this here old sad sack of a puss?" I said.

She opened her eyes and managed a smile. "Dear Ned," she said, barely able to use her voice.

"Hello, Jeanne," I said, fighting to manufacture my own smile and not drip tears. "What's new since we traded letters?"

"I'm dying, Ned."

"Silly girl, that's no way to talk."

"You mustn't tell Swaney and McDukes."

"Of course not."

They had missed seeing her on their one pass through Tap Dance years ago. For whatever her reasons, Jeanne didn't want either knowing her whereabouts and made me promise never to tell. I respected her wish as much as I respected the lady.

"Neither one, Ned, you understand?"

"Neither one, Jeanne."

"Not Swaney and not McDukes, Ned. Promise?"

"Promise."

"Do you know where they are now?"

I told her what I sensed she wanted to hear: "Still out there, Jeanne. Still breathing heavy and riding hard to somewhere, like always, chasing after a new adventure."

"Yes," she said to my lie, then closed her eyes and pretended to die.

A part of me pretended, too, and, rising to leave, I said, "Save a place for me."

ABOUT THE AUTHOR

Robert S. Levinson, award-winning, best-selling author of thirteen crime-thrillers, considered *Tap Dance,* his first Western novel, as homage to the cowboy movies and Saturday matinee serials of his boyhood. His short stories appeared regularly in the *Ellery Queen* and *Alfred Hitchcock* mystery magazines. He was a Derringer Award winner, multiple Shamus Award finalist, three-time *Ellery Queen* Readers Award choice, and was frequently included in "year's best" anthologies. His nonfiction appeared in *Rolling Stone, Los Angeles Times* Magazine, *Written By* Magazine of the Writers Guild of America, *Westways,* and *Los Angeles* Magazine. He served four years on Mystery Writers of America's (MWA) national board of directors, and wrote and produced two MWA annual "Edgar Awards" shows and two International Thriller Writers "Thriller Awards" shows.

The employees of Thorndike Press hope you have enjoyed this Large Print book. All our Thorndike, Wheeler, and Kennebec Large Print titles are designed for easy reading, and all our books are made to last. Other Thorndike Press Large Print books are available at your library, through selected bookstores, or directly from us.

For information about titles, please call:

(800) 223-1244

or visit our Web site at:

http://gale.cengage.com/thorndike

To share your comments, please write:

Publisher
Thorndike Press
10 Water St., Suite 310
Waterville, ME 04901